HELD BY T

Book 3 of the SW

Bella Drake

This is a work of fiction. The characters and events described herein are imaginary and are not intended to refer to specific places or to living persons alive or dead. All rights reserved. No part of this publication may be reproduced, distributed, or transmitted in any form or by any means, including photocopying, recording, or other electronic or mechanical methods without the prior written permission of the publisher except for brief quotations embodied in critical reviews.

Cover by TheBookBrander.com

Copyright © 2022 by Bella Drake

All rights reserved.

Also by Bella Drake

SWAT Shifter Series

WANTED BY THE WOLF

GUARDED BY THE GRIZZLY

HELD BY THE HAWK

PRIZED BY THE POLAR BEAR

PROTECTED BY THE PANTHER

Chapter One

Ramon

When his mom let out a string of curse words in Spanish, Ramon tried to hide his grin. His mother was one of the most patient people he'd ever known, but the fledglings were testing even her limits. Big time.

"Carlos, Antonio, Luis! You shift back into your human form this second!" his mother ordered. "And stop showing off in front of your cousins!"

Carlos flapped his wings a few times before the air around his tiny body shimmered. A few moments later, he was standing in the yard beaming, as naked as the day he was born. A couple of the younger girls tittered as Rosa hurriedly grabbed Carlos's clothes and thrust them at him.

"Get dressed," she commanded before turning to Gabriel, Ramon's brother and Carlos's father, and letting out a stream of rapid-fire Spanish.

Gabriel looked suitably chastised, then shouted at his son to put his clothes back on and stop messing around.

The young girls laughed harder, and the smile tugging at the corners of Ramon's mouth widened and he let out an amused chuckle.

Gabriel glared at him. "I'll remember this when Mom is shouting at you for something your kids have done."

"*My* kids!" Ramon spluttered. "You'll be waiting a long time for that, trust me."

"Don't be so sure about that, your mate could be just around the corner."

"Yeah, and she can stay there, too."

Ramon and his brother shared a chuckle over the joke just as their mom got back to them, all smiles again.

"Mi hijo," she said, sidling up to Ramon. "You never come over for dinner anymore."

Ramon winced. "I've been busy with work, Mama, you know that."

Rosa glared at him. "So busy you can't come and visit your lonely old mother? What's the name of your boss? I call him for you—tell him not to work you so hard. You need to spend time with your family."

Ramon had just taken a sip of his soda and it erupted from his mouth in a spluttering cough. He could only imagine how well Flint would take that. He'd never hear the end of it. And he was under no illusions; she'd call him. No doubt about it. When he chanced a glance at his brother, Gabriel had a satisfied grin on his lips.

"Asshole," he muttered.

His mother hit him upside the head.

"No swearing in my house," she chastised before letting out another string of curse words in Spanish.

Ramon rolled his eyes. "Don't let dad hear you refer to yourself as a lonely old woman, will you? Where is he, anyway?" He twisted round, as if the old man would peel himself from the woodwork, but he hadn't seen him for the better part of an hour.

"He had to leave. Flock business. And don't change the subject."

Ramon sighed. "I'll come to dinner next week, okay?"

Rosa's face became so animated anyone watching would have thought she'd won the lottery. Twice.

"Thank you, mi hijo. I make your favorite—tamales."

"Great."

"And I invite Louisa."

Ramon narrowed his eyes suspiciously. "Didn't Louisa's daughter just graduate college?"

"Yes!" Rosa said. "Good thinking. I invite her, too."

"No, wait, I didn't—"

"Carlos! Put your cousin down!" Rosa shouted before striding across the lawn to break up what looked like a competition between the two ten-year-olds to see who was the strongest.

"I walked right into that one, didn't I?" Ramon groused.

Gabriel grinned. "Fell for it hook, line, and sinker."

"When is she going to stop setting me up on dates?"

"You know she's hoping that one of them is your mate."

Ramon rolled his eyes. "Louisa's daughter has been coming around here since she was in diapers. Does mom think if we were mates that we wouldn't have realized it by now?"

"She lives in hope. Perhaps she thinks you just need another sniff of each other. You know she's a hopeless romantic. She wants to see you settled."

"She wants more grandbabies is what she wants."

Gabriel snorted. "Like she hasn't got enough kids to shout at."

Ramon nodded to Gabriel's son. "Were *we* ever like that?"

"Christ, I hope not."

Ramon laughed.

"You know, I ran into Mason Brown the other day."

Ramon felt the feathers around his neck ruffle just at the name. Their family had been at war with the Browns for as long as either side could remember. Big cat shifters and bird shifters were never going to get along, but it was more than just species. The animosity passed down through the family as readily as brown eyes and black hair. He narrowed his eyes and felt the tension rippling along his broad shoulders.

"Yeah? What did that reprobate have to say for himself?"

Gabriel chuckled. "He warned me to stay out of their territory."

Ramon's eyebrows rose. "You were in their corner of the city?"

There was a fragile peace, and it held because the two families avoided each other like the plague. Staying out of each other's breathing space kept the animosity spilling over into open war. Most of the time.

Gabriel rolled his eyes. "I work right around the corner from the boundary line and my boss asked me to pick something up for him on my lunch break. What was I supposed to do? Tell him no because, 'Surprise! I'm a hawk shifter whose family has been in a long-standing feud with a lion pride, and I'm not supposed to enter their territory?'" Gabriel blew out an exasperated breath and gesticulated with his hands, carving through the air in frustration. "He's human, he'd have laughed me out of the office and that would be after he called the men in white coats. There are only so many times I can refuse to do things for him before he, you know, fires me."

"Fair enough. And that was it, Mason just warned you? He didn't try to start anything?"

"No, unbelievably."

"Huh."

"Perhaps he was in a hurry."

"Yeah, maybe."

Ramon and Mason had come to blows on more than one occasion, their arguments often escalating into full-blown fist fights. His own flock, even his own father, had warned him to keep his distance, and he'd tried. Really, he had. It was just that the idiot had kept crossing his path like a bad penny. Mason was the son of the pride's dominant male, and the way he swaggered around, anyone would think that it was *Mason* who led the pride. Ramon didn't have the time of day for his ego. His own father was the leader of their flock, but Ramon wouldn't have been caught dead throwing his weight around the way Mason did. But he wasn't about to back down from him, either. Besides, he figured they were equally matched in size, strength, and rank, if not in intellect. Mason was about five IQ points above an ignoramus. On a good day.

It had been a few years since Ramon had last seen Mason, which could only be considered a good thing, not least by his mom who still seemed to think he was a little kid who needed to be kept out of trouble. When he'd been younger, Ramon had been hot-tempered and had thought nothing about getting into a fight with Mason or any of the males in the pride, but despite what his family thought, he *had* grown up. He worked for the FBI now, as a member of their elite SWAT team, and he'd worked hard to get there. Hard enough that he wasn't about to throw it all away by getting involved in stupid scuffles—his job meant everything to him. Hawk, as he was known to his teammates, was the sharpshooter, and he loved what he did with a passion. There was nothing he would rather have been doing. Not even taking Mason Brown down a peg or two.

"Are you talking about Mason Brown?" Felipe, Ramon's cousin, asked as he joined them at the tail end of their conversation.

Ramon nodded. "You know him?"

"Yeah, unfortunately. Guy's a real piece of work."

Gabriel snorted. "You got that right."

"My younger brother has gone to Mason's house tonight, actually. Idiot."

Ramon froze. "Say again?"

"Yeah, he went with a couple of his friends. The Browns are having a party for Mason's sister or some such. I warned him to stay away, but he wouldn't hear of it—said they weren't going to start trouble, just for shits and giggles."

"The damn fools will get themselves killed," Ramon ground out. Keeping the peace was hard enough when both sides wanted it.

All the color drained out of Felipe's face. "You don't think they'd get seriously hurt, do you?"

"They're adolescents," Ramon spat. "What do you think?"

Felipe frowned. "Well, sure, but they wouldn't cause any real trouble, they're not that stupid."

"They're hawk shifters," Ramon said. "Who are walking right into the lion's den. Literally. How long do think they'll last before they're found out? What if they get into an argument and get het up and shift? They'll be torn apart."

"Oh God, I didn't think about that."

Ramon shook his head and exhaled heavily. Idiots or not, he couldn't let them get hurt. They were still family. Apparently. "Do you know the address of the party?"

Felipe nodded. "Carlos tried to get me to take them there, but I told him I didn't want any part in it."

At least one member of this family had some sense. "I'm going to get the fools before they start something they can't get out of."

Gabriel frowned. "I'd come with you, but I've got to take Carlos home and pick Angela up from her shift at the hospital on the way."

"You don't need to explain," Ramon said. "Anyway, it's better if you don't come. We don't need any more hawk shifters there than absolutely necessary. The last thing any of us need is them getting it into their heads that we're declaring war."

"You can't go alone," Gabriel said.

"I could come with you," Felipe suggested.

Ramon shook his head. "Same deal. I'll call one of my SWAT buddies, see if he can ride shotgun."

Ramon pulled out his cellphone then scrolled through his phone book to find the right number. His friend picked up after a couple of rings.

"Hawk?" Nash greeted him. "Everything okay?"

"Yeah. Well, not really. You remember that favor you said I could ask of you?"

The one Ramon had chalked up a few months ago by looking into the bear shifter's mate's husband—which was all kinds of messed up by itself—who used to work for one of the cartels. Ramon hadn't minded doing it—Diego was bad to the bone. He'd had never intended to collect on the favor, but a bunch of hawk shifter kids walking into the heart of lion territory changed things.

"Name it," Nash said, without hesitation.

"My cousin has got himself into a situation and I need to go and rescue him before the idiot gets himself killed. I'd appreciate some backup."

"Now?"

"Yeah, can you do it?"

"Of course. Already on my way. You want me to meet you there?"

Ramon felt a weight lift from his shoulders. It was the true sign of a friend that Nash would agree to help him out, no questions asked. But then Ramon would have done the same thing for any of his SWAT teammates, too. They were more than just his colleagues; they were his extended family. Each member of the team was a different shifter species and it occurred to Ramon that if *they* could all get along so well, why couldn't his flock learn to get along with the pride? It also occurred to him that he didn't have time to waste on philosophy right now.

"Uh, no. I'll pick you up. Then I can fill you in on the details on the way."

"Sure thing. I'll text you my address."

"Appreciate ya."

Ramon went to tell his mom he was leaving the party then headed out, hoping he could get there and get the boys out before anyone at the party realized who they were and really did declare war.

Chapter Two

Saffy

Seraphina Brown looked around at the excitable young shifters and fought to hide her scowl. It was her sister's sweet sixteenth and she'd never have heard the end of it if she didn't show, but that didn't make it any more bearable. All around her, relationships were being formed and broken, couples held hands and made out, then argued and broke up, moving onto someone new before the DJ had started playing the next tune.

How could a bunch of teenagers have a better dating life than she had at twenty-six? She just couldn't understand it. She heaved a sigh. Actually, she *could* understand it. She knew the reason for her lack of romantic entanglements, of course she did. She'd had relationships in the past, but a shadow had hung over all of them, and whenever she'd started to really fall for them, she'd done the only sensible thing, and broken it off. It was better that way. Before anyone could get too attached, and too badly hurt.

She'd had to.

What would have happened if she'd found her mate? People could get destroyed. No relationship could ever hope to compete with the pull of the mate bond. No way, no how. And how was she supposed to live with herself if she spent years with someone, made a life with them, a home, and then broke it off with those four words that most shifters longed to say... *I've met my mate.*

No. She couldn't put someone through that, and even if she never met her mate, she couldn't spend every day looking at a man she loved, wondering if that would be the day some quirk of fate would strip everything away. It was better to call things off before she fell even deeper and spent years of her life with someone who was just a fill in until the real deal came along. That wouldn't have been fair on either of them. And every breakup broke *her* just a little bit more, so that now any form of dating worried her, in case she fell that bit too hard.

Relationships were off the table for her, and it was better that way.

It kind of made sense, in her head at least, but her libido had other ideas. She wished she was the type of woman who could be content with anonymous hook-ups with strangers she met online, but she couldn't go for that. She was too old-fashioned. She wanted hearts and flowers—romance, not a quick fumble in a car with some guy who had probably taken off his wedding ring five minutes before meeting with her. Men like that made her feel queasy—as did her brother's friend Leon, who had been checking her out all night.

Yet another reason she wished she could be anywhere but here right now.

The salacious glances he kept throwing her way were enough to make her lose her dinner, but it had been even worse when he'd come to talk to her earlier. The lust he'd been throwing off in waves had tickled her nose and tested her gag reflex. Usually, scenting a shifter's lust would be enough to make her inner cat purr, but with him, it had the opposite effect. It made her cat's claws threaten to elongate and made the human side of her desperate to take a long, hot shower. The crazy thing was, he had no idea how repulsive she found him. No clue whatsoever. He thought he was God's gift. She'd even seen him eying up some of her sister's friends. They were *sixteen* years old.

What the hell was wrong with him?

Saffy wasn't keen on Jason, her brother's other friend, either, but at least he didn't try to get in her pants at every given opportunity. That had to count for something. Her brother, Jason, and Leon had been thick as thieves for as long as Saffy could remember, but it was only in recent years that Leon had taken such a shine to her, which had at least spared her a few years of his unwelcome interest, she supposed.

When she saw the man in question heading her way again, Saffy panicked, looking around for somewhere she could hide. In the end, she pretended her sister was calling her and hurried over to where Charlotte was standing around talking with a small group of her friends.

"Quick," she muttered under her breath. "Hide me. If I have to talk to Leon again, I won't be responsible for my actions."

Her sister wrinkled her nose. "Do you mean Mason's friend? Yeah, he's gross."

Charlotte's friends all nodded and muttered their agreement, and Saffy's eyes narrowed.

"He hasn't tried anything on with any of you, has he?" she asked. If he'd said so much as a single inappropriate word to any of them, she'd have his head, and to hell with the consequences.

"No," Charlotte replied. "But he looks at us like we're a piece of meat."

"Stay away from him," Saffy warned. "I don't even know what he's doing here."

"Blame Mom. She said that you and Mason had to chaperone tonight, and Mason told her he wouldn't do it unless he could bring his two partners in crime."

"Huh, figures. Seems like they're all joined at the hip lately, even more so than usual." She shook her head and forced a bright smile. This was supposed to be a birthday celebration, after all. "Anyway, are you enjoying the party?"

A tentative smile slid over Charlotte's lips. "Yeah, it's cool, but I hate that everyone keeps staring at me."

"It's because you look so hot," Saffy said, causing her sister and her friends to break out into a round of giggles.

Saffy wasn't surprised her sister was uncomfortable. Charlotte had always been a shy, quiet child. She was reserved and introverted, often preferring to be in her own company rather than be around a group of people. She'd never liked being the center of attention, so being the star of a sweet sixteenth had to be hell for her. Charlotte hadn't even wanted the party, but their mom had insisted. She'd said it was a rite of passage, but Saffy knew the real reason was so she could show off to the pride.

"Is he gone?" Saffy asked.

Charlotte looked covertly over Saffy's shoulder, then nodded. "Yeah, he's with Mason again. He's not looking over here."

Saffy breathed a sigh of relief. "Thank God for that. So, you got your eye on anyone here?"

Saffy shook her head, but one of her friends ratted her out. "She likes Ethan Johnson."

Charlotte glared at her friend, and Saffy hid a smile, instead putting on her most suspicious and protective face.

"Oh really?" Saffy said. "And just who is this Ethan Johnson? Do I need to have a word with him?"

When her sister's eyes nearly bugged out of her head, Saffy decided to put her out of her misery.

"I'm only messing with you. I wouldn't really say anything to him. Where is he, anyway? Is he a looker? I bet he is."

Saffy glanced around at the boys in the party and her gaze landed on a particularly rowdy trio. "He's not one of those boys, is he?" she asked, nodding in their direction.

The girls burst out in fits of giggles. "No," one of her friends said. "They are *hawk* shifters."

Saffy snorted. "Right."

"No, really," Charlotte said. "They gatecrashed."

Saffy froze. "*What*? Why didn't you come and tell me?"

Charlotte shrugged and scuffed her feet.

"Damn it. I'd better throw them out before your brother finds out they're here. He's had a lot to drink and you know how much he hates the Miguel family."

Charlotte frowned. "He wouldn't hurt them, would he?"

Saffy sighed. "Um, probably not, no. Nothing to worry about. I'll sort it."

Saffy strode across the yard with purpose, hoping that Leon didn't turn around and make a beeline for her. She hadn't exactly been telling her sister the truth, because if Mason found out there were hawk shifters present, he would lose his shit. And he most definitely *would* hurt them, even though they only looked about sixteen and

Mason had over a decade on them. They weren't called a pride of lions for nothing, and much as she loved her brother, his ego had led him to cause trouble more than once. And tonight was most definitely not the night for bloodshed. Once, just once, it'd be nice if the family could have a normal, peaceful party.

She stopped in front of the three boys and one of them turned to look at her. As he did, his eyes started to shift, and the pupil was abnormally large. He got himself under control quickly—most likely he'd been using his shifter senses to scrutinize her—but she'd seen all she needed to. It was a sure sign of his species. They were hawk shifters, alright.

"All right, boys, you've had your fun," Saffy said. "Now it's time for you to leave."

The tallest boy puffed out his chest. "Yeah, who's going to make us?"

Saffy glared at him. Her father was the dominant male of their pride which made her incredibly dominant, too. She let her guard down a little and let a little of that alpha power color her voice when she replied.

"*I* will."

All three boys widened their eyes and either consciously or unconsciously leaned away from her. Unfortunately, they recovered from her display quickly and a mask of teenaged bravado covered their faces again.

"Yeah, you and what army?"

Saffy ground her teeth together. She'd have to try harder to put the fear of God into them, before Mason sent them to *meet* their god.

"You see those three men over there?" she asked, pointing to her brother, Leon, and Jason, and uttering a silent prayer that they didn't turn round and see her confronting the hawk shifters before they took the hint and left of their own free will.

The hawk shifters nodded in unison.

"Well, that's Mason Brown, the dominant's son, with his two best friends. You heard of him?"

They nodded, their eyes wider still.

"Good. Because I'm here to tell you that everything you've heard about him is probably true. Mason is meaner than a snake and trust me, you do not want to get on the wrong side of him. Understand?"

All three boys studied him closely, then a smirk slid over the lips of the tallest.

"I could take him," he said.

The boy's two friends guffawed loudly, drawing the attention of a few shifters nearby.

Damn it all to hell. Saffy had hoped that merely pointing out her brother was present at the party would be enough to get the boys to leave, but they weren't budging. She had to hand it to them, they had balls the size of melons. Either that or they were incredibly stupid. Well, they were juveniles, so it was probably the latter. Male adolescent shifters had a bit of a god complex until they got in a fight or two with someone stronger than them and they realized they weren't invincible. Clearly, that had yet to happen to these boys. Unfortunately it was going to, and soon, if they didn't see some sense.

"Yeah, we could kick their asses," one of the taller boy's friends said.

This remark was made so loudly that Saffy winced and chanced a look over her shoulder to make sure Mason and his friends hadn't overhead all the way across the yard.

"Will you shut the hell up?" she snapped. "Jesus, do you boys have a death wish? Do you really want to start a fight here? You know there are over thirty male lions here, right? They would love nothing more than to get their hands on a few dumbass Miguels. And that's not to mention the lionesses here who could also kick your asses in their sleep."

Damn it. That had been the wrong thing to say. Saffy realized it as soon as the words had fallen from her lips. It had been bad enough to imply that any of the male lions present could take them in a fight, but to then suggest that even the lionesses could best them was a serious blow to their male pride. Even if it was true. Ugh. Fragile male egos, it felt like they were the bane of her life. Certainly the bane of her evening. Male shifters were ridiculously sensitive about things like that—even more than the average human male, which was why she tended not to date shifters on the rare occasions she gave it a go. She'd insulted the boys. Badly. She should have kept her mouth shut. In fact, she shouldn't even be arguing with them at all. She was the adult. She should have known better.

The tallest boy was so angry his body began to vibrate, signaling the onset of a shift. A moment later, a fine dusting of feathers covered his forearms.

"Oh, now you've gone and done it, lady!" one of the boy's friends groaned.

"I'm sorry for saying that," she told him quietly, calmly. "Just relax, will you? Everything's going to be all right. You just need to calm down."

"I could take on anyone here!" the boy roared. "*Anyone!*"

Well, hell. There went her plans for keeping their presence under wraps. If she didn't handle this quickly and carefully, her sister's party would descend into chaos—a dangerous brawl at best, a bloodbath at worst. Perhaps she should go and call her father to come and handle the situation. He and her mother were watching movies in their bedroom with the door locked so they couldn't be disturbed. Her mother had wanted them to be close at hand in case they were needed, but out of sight so that the presence of the dominant male wasn't a deterrent for the kids to have fun. This felt like the kind of situation her father would want to be alerted to. Saffy was just about to run up to call him when a voice stopped her in her tracks.

"What the fuck is this?" her brother said from over her shoulder.

Saffy winced then spun around to face him.

"Now, Mason," she said. "Leave them alone, okay? They're just kids."

"We're not *kids*!" the boy shouted.

Saffy closed her eyes. For crying out loud. She'd done it again. What the heck was wrong with her? No, wait, what the heck was wrong with *them?* And there she'd been thinking that being overly sensitive about someone pointing out their age was a woman's prerogative, but she had the sense to keep that thought to herself, while there was still at least some chance of this evening ending without bloodshed. But really, what the hell was the Miguel family teaching their kids? They ought to raise them to have at least a little more sense.

A toothy grin spread across Mason's lips, one that was full of menace.

"You heard what they said, sis, they're not kids." Mason grinned. "Well, if they want to be treated like adults, they can get their asses kicked liked adults, too."

Leon and Jason had taken up a flanking position behind Saffy's brother and chuckled at his poor excuse for a joke.

"Please, Mason," she said. "Don't start anything. Not tonight, not here at Charlotte's party."

"I didn't start a fucking thing," Mason slurred, making Saffy groan inwardly. That was what she needed—a drunk, testosterone fueled Mason who thought his family had been insulted. Excellent. Tonight just kept getting better and better.

"*They* started it by trespassing on private property. Who the fuck do they think they are?" He shouldered around her and got up in the boy's faces. "Who the *fuck* do you think you are?"

Saffy uttered a prayer that they would finally develop some belated sense and keep their mouths shut.

"We're Miguels!" the tallest boy replied. "Who the fuck do you think *you* are?"

And so much for that. Figured that it had been too much to hope for. And now his idiotic reply had undoubtedly sealed the boy's fate. There was only one way this could end. Her sister's party was about to go to hell in a handbasket and she had serious concerns for the safety of the trio of teenagers. She needed to alert her father, but if she left now, there would be no one who would dare stand up to her brother. She looked around to try to get her sister's attention, but she couldn't see her anywhere. Saffy was on her own. Just great.

Chapter Three

Ramon

Even if he hadn't known the address where the party was being held, it would have been obvious when they arrived on the street. Music was blaring out of the largest house on the road by far, and some of the partygoers had spilled out onto the large, immaculate front yard. Ramon parked along the curb opposite and cut the engine.

"And into the lion's den we go," he murmured.

Nash chuckled. "Bet you feel safer knowing you've got a big strong bear to protect you, don't you, huh?"

Ramon barked out a laugh. "You might be about ten times as big as me in shifted form, but my hawk could still kick your bear's ass in a fight."

Nash snorted. "In your dreams. It'd be like swatting a fly. One swipe and you'd be done for."

"Perhaps," Ramon conceded. "But you'd have to get that swipe in first and you'd have no chance of getting anywhere near me. I'd be ten times faster than your slow ass."

"Sounds like a challenge," Nash said.

"Any day, any way, my friend."

They laughed good-naturedly as they made their way around the back of the property. Unfortunately, any hope Ramon had held onto about grabbing the boys and getting out unnoticed disappeared when he heard the raised voices in the backyard.

"*They* started it by trespassing on private property. Who the fuck do they think they are?" And a moment later, "Who the *fuck* do you think you are?"

"Shit, quick," Ramon said, breaking into a run.

He would have recognized that voice anywhere—Mason Brown. And he sounded drunk. Ramon's heart plummeted when he heard one of the boys reply, "We're Miguels! Who the fuck do you think *you* are?"

Stupid goddamn idiots. What in the hell did they think they were playing at? If they made it out of this alive, Ramon was going to kill them. He ran into the backyard in time to see the look of incredulity on Mason's face. Then the man brought back his arm, hand clenched into a fist.

"Mason!" Ramon shouted to get his attention.

Mason turned at the sound of his name being called, distracting him from the punch he'd been about to land, but upon seeing Ramon, his face lit up with predatory glee.

"Only you would be dumb enough to wander into a lion's den," Mason said around a cackle. "Oh, and these fools right here, of course. These your sidekicks, are they?"

"We're no one's *sidekicks*," Carlos spat.

"*Carlos*!" Ramon shouted. "Shut the hell up!"

The boy looked annoyed at being spoken to like that, but he knew better than to answer back to Ramon. Most kids did. Ramon would have liked to have thought it was because he worked for the FBI or because of the reputation he'd built as a fair but tough adjudicator of the family's minor spats, but he was under no illusions. It was more likely to be because his father was leader of the flock. None of them wanted to get their asses tossed out.

Ramon drew his shoulders back and started towards the small cluster. He drew in a deep breath, readying himself to defuse the situation, when a scent hit him out of nowhere, so powerful it nearly caused him to faceplant on the fancy wooden decking. What the hell? It wasn't, as he'd have expected surrounded by a pride of belligerent lions, the scent of decay or decadence. In fact, it wasn't an unpleasant scent at all. Quite the opposite. It was divine—like spring roses and fresh cut hay. He tried to take another step forward but stumbled. Nash, who had fallen in line beside him, cocked his head to one side and studied him.

"Hawk? You okay, buddy? You don't look so good."

Mason roared with laughter. "He looks like he's gonna puke."

"Smell," Ramon managed to choke out.

Nash screwed his face up in confusion. "Huh?"

"Smell," he said again. "Oh, shit."

At that, Nash looked even more perturbed. "I don't smell shit, wait, did *you* shit?"

Ramon closed his eyes and prayed for strength. Trouble was, with his eyes closed, the scent seemed even more intense. Intoxicating. He needed to find its source. He opened his eyes again just as they shifted into his hawk form and his fingernails lengthened into talons.

"Oh, the party just got *real* interesting," Mason said. "Bring it on."

"Mason, *don't*," a soft, feminine voice ordered.

Ramon's head swung in her direction, and it was like staring into the face of an angel. She was so beautiful that he was tempted to shield his eyes, as if her beauty might blind him. Already he knew he never wanted to look on anything but her for the rest of his life. Her long, pale blonde hair looked as if it had been spun from pure sunshine and her big blue eyes were as light as the sky on a summer's day.

"Mine," he breathed.

"Oh, shit," Nash groaned.

It was only a small consolation, but the woman looked as awestruck as Ramon felt. As he stared, her eyes shifted, and sharp looking incisors tore down past her lips.

"What the fuck? He's in a daze," Mason slurred. "Is he high?"

When Mason stumbled his way, Ramon tore his gaze away from the beautiful goddess and fought for control. This wasn't a good time to lose his shit, not if he liked his head on his shoulders—Mason Brown would be more than happy to knock it off and use it as a soccer ball. Ramon needed to have his wits about him. And it probably wouldn't have been a good idea to tell him that the woman who had just addressed him and was more than likely a cat shifter like Mason, judging by the size of her incisors, was Ramon's fated mate.

Wait a minute. She hadn't just addressed Mason, she'd *commanded* him. Who in their right mind would speak to Mason Brown that way? She had to have known him very damn well to speak to the son of the dominant male that way, a man who himself was incredibly dominant, if as dumb as a box of hammers. Who was she to him? Was she...his girlfriend? Rage unlike anything Ramon had experienced tore through his body like wildfire and he felt the need to pummel something, preferably Mason's face. Inside, his bird squawked and clawed, desperate to be set free.

Mine. Mine. Not his. She's mine.

Tingles started at the base of Ramon's neck and feathers sprouted. He tried to calm down and think logically, but his brain evidently wasn't firing on all cylinders. Every calming breath he drew in only sucked more of her intoxicating scent into his lungs to fuel the jealous rage burning through him. *Think, think,* he urged himself, a counterpoint to his hawk's steady cry of *mine, mine.*

Maybe she was just a member of the pride, albeit a high ranking one. No, there weren't many shifters who could speak to a dominant's eldest son like that and expect to get away unscathed, especially when that son was Mason.

Won't let anyone harm our mate, his hawk seethed.

Perhaps they were related? He didn't like the idea of her being part of this Neanderthal's family, but it was better than the alternative.

"Did you think you could come here and ruin my sister's birthday party?" Mason shouted. "Well, if you're looking for a fight, then you came to the right place."

"We're not here to fight," Nash said calmly. "That's the God's honest truth. We just came to get those three fools."

"Bullshit," Mason spat. "You probably brought them. What, did you think the five of you stood a chance against all of us?"

The three young juveniles were standing behind Mason and shooting glares at Mason's friends. The friends, Leon and Jason if Ramon remembered correctly, were goading the boys something fierce. If Ramon didn't do something quickly, one of them was going to snap. All it would take was for one punch to be thrown and all hell would break loose.

Ramon's gaze moved to the woman again and it was evident that she, too, was trying to get herself back under control. She had managed to shift her eyes back to their human form, but she'd had no such luck with her incisors, which were still visible between her parted lips. It was the hottest damn thing that Ramon had ever seen.

One of Mason's friends said something, but Ramon was so focused on the woman's captivating presence, he didn't hear what it was.

"Shut your goddamn mouth!" Carlos shouted at him.

Before Ramon could do anything to prevent it, Carlos slammed his fist into Leon's face and the sickening sound of bone breaking carried even over the din of the music.

"Oh shit," Ramon and Nash said in unison.

Mason spun around and roared, lunging for Carlos, who deftly managed to sidestep him. Leon recovered quickly from the punch, too quickly, and snatched up a fistful of the neck of Carlos's shirt. Carlos squirmed, but the lion shifter's strength held the teenager in place while he threw a punch of his own. It caught one of Carlos' cheeks, right below his eye, and blood immediately erupted.

This had gone too far.

"FBI!" Ramon shouted, pulling out his badge in the hopes that the sight of it would be a deterrent for the men and make then stop fighting. No such luck. The three of them completely ignored him and it and rounded on the three young hawk shifters.

"Goddamn it." Ramon and Nash moved into the fray. "FBI!" Ramon said again as he took hold of Mason's arm to prevent him from throwing a punch.

Instead, Mason swung his body around and punched Ramon with his other hand, the impact making his neck snap back on his shoulders.

"That's it," Ramon growled. "I'm arresting you for assaulting a federal officer."

Mason threw his head back and laughed as Ramon unclipped the handcuffs off his belt. He turned to share his amusement with his two friends, and Ramon moved in quickly, grabbing his wrists and snapping the cuffs shut around them. Mason's amusement evaporated immediately.

"What the fuck!" Mason shouted, straining against the cuffs.

"I warned you, Mason," Ramon said.

The sight of Mason in handcuffs stopped Jason and Leon in their tracks. They froze, their eyes wide in alarm.

"They're FBI?" Leon said. "I thought he was just saying that."

Ramon heaved a sigh. "Ted?" he said using Nash's SWAT team nickname. "Can you put Ramon in my car, please?"

"Sure thing."

Nash pulled an arguing, struggling Mason along behind him, leaving Ramon alone with the small gathering. He looked across at the woman again then frowned. This was *not* how he had envisioned meeting his mate. She glared at him, and it was like someone driving a lance through his gut. Damn. She must have taken his frown the wrong way. But how could she possibly think he was frowning at *her?* He'd talk to her, as soon as he got the chance. First, he turned to Mason's two friends.

"Get out of my sight," he said. "Before I arrest you, too, for assaulting a minor."

They hotfooted it away without another word.

"And you three," Ramon fumed, staring at the three fool hawk shifters in turn. "What in the hell did you think you were playing at, coming here tonight?"

"We just wanted to have some fun," Carlos said.

"You just wanted to start some trouble is what you wanted. How did you get here?"

One of Carlos' friends stepped forward. Ramon thought his name was Santino. "I borrowed my dad's car, sir."

"Well get back in it and get home. *Straight* home," Ramon ordered. "Before I arrest you three idiots as well. If I find out you went anywhere else after leaving here, there'll be hell to pay. Do I make myself clear?"

They nodded.

"Answer me," Ramon thundered.

"Yes, sir!" they all said quickly.

"Now get. And I'll see all three of you tomorrow."

They practically ran from the yard, leaving Ramon finally standing alone with his mate not ten feet away from him. He stumbled closer, hoping he wouldn't trip over his tongue as well as his feet.

"*Mate*," he breathed again.

"It would seem that way, yes," she replied. "It would seem that you're also not happy about that fact. In the least."

"No, I am," Ramon was quick to assure her. "I mean, I never thought I would meet my mate under such circumstances, but I am happy."

He frowned when something occurred to him. She'd said *also*.

"Aren't you? Happy, I mean."

She heaved a sigh. "You're a hawk shifter."

"And you're a lion."

"It's impossible," she said. "My family already hates yours. And now that you've arrested my brother…"

"Your *brother*?"

The fact made Ramon both elated and thoroughly dejected at the same time.

"I'm sorry about that. It was the only way I could get them to stop fighting."

"You're an FBI agent?"

"Yes, on a SWAT team." It was impossible to keep the trace of pride from his voice when he said it.

Yes, his bird urged. *Impress mate with our titles.*

"Assaulting a federal agent," she murmured. "Mason will go to prison for that, probably for a long time." She shook her head. "Not that the little shit doesn't deserve it."

Ramon couldn't help himself, a booming laugh tore from his throat. He quickly reined it in, but he couldn't quite keep the amusement from his face.

"I see even Mason's family aren't immune to his many…er, charms."

She grinned. "How did you guess?"

"Look, don't worry. I'll tell my superior I only arrested Mason to get him to calm down. There won't be any repercussions, okay?"

A cute little crease settled on her forehead. "You'd do that for him?"

"No." He shook his head. "I'd do it for you."

She smiled at him and Ramon's heart stuttered.

"Thank you."

"Look, can we—"

"*Saffy?*" a man's voice called.

Ramon's mate gasped, then turned to look over her shoulder. "Father."

Ramon looked across at the intruder, annoyed at having his first conversation with his mate interrupted, only to find himself face to face with Owen Brown, the dominant male leader of the lion pride.

"What's going on?" Owen asked. "Where's your brother? And why is *he* here?"

Ramon hadn't had what he might call a run in with Owen in the past, but he'd been forced to speak to the man about members of his pride when he was on official FBI business and the man had treated him with contempt, even though Ramon had been nothing but civil to him. Well, mostly.

"I'd better go," Ramon said.

He leaned closer to…Saffy, was that her name? He liked it. It was fiery, yet beautiful. Like her.

"Do you know where the FBI headquarters are in the city?"

"Yes."

"Come there in an hour and I'll have Mason released. You can pick him up. Okay?"

She smiled gratefully. "I will. Thank you."

He nodded. "My name's Ramon, by the way. See you soon."

He could hardly wait.

Chapter Four

Saffy

Saffy's heart thudded as she maneuvered her convertible Mercedes down the into the bowels of the FBI's underground parking lot. She couldn't believe she was about to see her mate again. The last hour had been the longest of her life.

It had taken every bit of persuasion that she possessed to prevent her father from coming to pick Mason up himself. He wanted to give Ramon a piece of his mind and talk to his superiors to see if he could get the man arrested for trespassing on private property. If it was up to her father, he'd have got Ramon fired from his job, too. Saffy had heard the pride in his voice when he'd spoken about being SWAT, and she wasn't about to let her father try to take that from him. Or anything else.

Her father hadn't believed that Ramon had just been there to pick up the three young hawk shifters. He maintained that Ramon had brought them there himself, just to cause trouble and so that he could arrest Mason.

Apparently he thought that Ramon was as incapable of letting go of old grudges as Mason was himself. She frowned. Maybe it was true. She didn't know anything about him, not really.

No. It *wasn't* true, she was sure of it. He'd tried to calm things down, and besides, there was no way he'd jeopardize his job just because they'd had a couple of scraps a few years ago. Just because her family—well, and his, apparently—were incapable of letting go of old grudges, didn't mean Ramon was.

Saffy had tried to reassure her father that he was mistaken, that Ramon had been furious at the three young shifters, but he hadn't wanted to hear it. He'd said Ramon was a good liar and that she was naïve to fall for it. And she'd heard the disappointment in his voice when he'd said it, like believing anything a hawk said made her less. Weak. And he'd never had any time for weakness.

She'd wanted to tell her father that Ramon was her mate, but it hadn't been the right time. Her father was already furious at the man—she would only have made things worse, so she stayed silent. But now she was thinking that she should have just told him and gotten it over with. She was pretty sure there wasn't ever going to be a good time to tell him her mate was a hawk shifter. And not just any hawk shifter, but the son of the leader of the flock, or so her father said. Still, it was hard to imagine there being a *worse* time, so maybe it was for the best.

She sighed and stared up at the roof of her car. When a shifter found their mate, it was supposed to be a happy occasion, one that all their friends and family supported and congratulated them on. Hell would freeze over before her father ever congratulated her on mating with a Miguel. He'd see it as the hawks taking something from them, stealing something—like a woman was something that could be stolen. Or a heart.

But she wouldn't have changed who her mate was, even if she could. She wasn't prejudiced against the Miguel family like her father and brother were. Why did species matter? No-one even seemed to know for sure how it had begun, and when a family of shifters with abnormally long lives couldn't trace its origin, maybe it was time to let it die.

Right. She was pretty sure the sun would die before that damn grudge.

Shaking her head—her father was right, she really was naïve—she got out of the car, and her heart started beating faster. His scent was all over this place, old and new. When she turned away from the car, she caught sight of a figure by the closed doors of an elevator at the far end of the parking lot. Ramon. She knew him even from this distance. She was pretty sure she'd know him in the pitch dark with her nostrils plugged. The mate bond sang to her.

Mate, her lion said, nodding its approval.

She smoothed down her skirt as she strode across the lot and couldn't quite keep the grin from her face as she approached him. Ramon's answering smile made her belly flutter. He was so handsome—unbelievably so. His square jaw had just a trace of dark stubble, and his shirt pulled tight across his shoulders, giving a hint of the broad muscles beneath. Her lion purred in satisfaction.

Mine.

"Hey," she greeted him, walking right up into his personal space.

"Hey, yourself."

He reached for her, his arms sliding around her back. He pulled her up against the hard lines of his body and she went to him willingly, sliding her hands over his shoulders. It felt like the most natural thing in the world to do and when he leaned forward and kissed her, her lips molded to his as if they'd been doing so for years.

The kiss was infinitely more than a friendly peck on the lips and when Ramon opened his mouth to deepen the kiss, she parted her lips to allow his tongue entrance. When his hands slid down to grip the cheeks of her ass, she shivered. How could her body ache for the touch of someone she'd only just met? It didn't make any sense, but at the same time, it made perfect sense. She'd felt desire for men before, even been in love, but none of them had been her mate. She'd been right to wait for him. What she'd felt before was just a faint echo of what she felt now. This was meant to be. It had nothing to do with her family or his and everything to do with what they were to one another—soul mates. Two bodies, two hearts, but one shared soul.

When they finally broke apart, they were breathing heavily, and Ramon's eyes had shifted to their bird form as hers had shifted to her cat's. Then her eyes zeroed in on his lips and the drop of blood she saw there. She gasped.

"Oh my gosh, did I cut you? I'm so sorry."

She hadn't realized until then that her incisors had lengthened, and they were incredibly sharp. She'd have to be more careful.

Ramon, who was wearing a sappy grin she couldn't help but find adorable, reached up and swiped the drop of blood away with his finger.

"Oh, this? It's nothing."

She sighed dreamily. "That was one hell of a greeting."

His grin broadened. "Wasn't it?"

"I hate to spoil the moment but, my brother?"

"Oh, right. He's just getting a bit of a talking to by my team leader then he'll be down. All charges have been dropped."

She nodded. "Good. Well, not good exactly. It would serve my brother right to spend some time in jail, but I don't want my father to dislike you anymore than he already does."

Though she was pretty sure *that* wasn't possible.

Ramon sighed. "I doubt my parents will be thrilled when they hear the news, either. According to my dad, the Brown family is the root of all evil."

"Funny, my dad says the same thing about the Miguels." She shook her head. "Stupid damn feud."

"Isn't it? Do you know what started it?"

Saffy shook her head. "Not exactly. Dad told me once that it was something to do with his father's sister getting killed and that a Miguel was responsible, but he would never tell me the full story. I don't think he even knows it."

"It was to do with my grandfather's brother," Ramon said. "Or at least, so my father says. They were in love, but my father said neither family was happy about their relationship because of their different species."

Saffy leaned in a closer, riveted to finally hear the details of what had started the argument between their families. "Go on."

"Well, apparently both sets of parents had forbidden them to see one another anymore, but they refused to listen and carried on seeing one another in secret."

"Okay."

A rumble of trepidation churned in her stomach. So far, it sounded like her own story, except they hadn't even had a grudge to contend with. Did it mean her own relationship with Ramon was doomed?

Ramon squeezed her hand, like he knew the thoughts that were plaguing her, and one side of his mouth lifted in a small, sad smile that made her heart flutter. They wouldn't repeat the mistakes of the past, whatever they were. They'd find a way to be together.

"They were in my great uncle's car one night when they saw her brother, your grandfather, in a car with his friends. They were in a rush to get away so that they wouldn't be found out, and my uncle's car skidded on a wet patch. He lost control and wrapped the car around a tree."

Saffy stared at him, rapt.

"She was killed on impact, and my granduncle was rushed into hospital with internal bleeding. Of course, being a shifter, he was able to heal quite quickly from his injuries."

"Oh, my," Saffy said, her hand covering her mouth.

Ramon nodded. "When my granduncle got out of the hospital, he ended his own life. He wrote in the suicide note that he wasn't able to live without his mate."

Saffy gasped. "They were mates?"

"Yes. Then, of course, your family blamed mine for the death of your grandfather's sister, and my family blamed yours for my great uncle's death. And so, the feud was born."

A tear escaped Saffy's eye and slowly slid down her cheek. "That's tragic."

"Yeah."

"The deaths should have made them come together, not driven an even bigger wedge between the two families."

"Yeah," he agreed. "But grief can make people act irrationally."

"And it was all because they were too stupid and prejudiced against a species different to their own." She couldn't keep the trace of bitterness from her voice. What did it matter what animal someone turned into? How could that be more important than finding your soul mate? If only their families could have been happy for them, their story could have ended so differently. Not in tragedy, but in love.

"I see a lot of prejudice and hate crimes in my line of work," Ramon said, and she caught her own hopelessness reflected in his tone as he stared over her shoulder. "It makes me think that as a society, we're not getting any better. If anything, we're regressing."

"You'd think shifters would know better. I mean, we're already hiding who we are from humans for fear of causing widespread panic, and now we're fighting amongst ourselves, too."

"It's pathetic, it really is," Ramon agreed.

Saffy put her hands on his shoulders. "Promise me you won't let our families come between us?"

"Never," Ramon said with conviction and the truth of that shone in his eyes, calming her and her cat who had become agitated after hearing the story of their relatives. "You're my mate. I'd never let anything get in the way of that."

Relief washed over Saffy like a balm to the anxiety that had her as on edge as her lion. She felt the conviction of their mate bond, and of course she'd hoped he would feel the way, but hearing him say it out loud relieved the pressure mounting inside her.

Ramon leaned closer, setting her heart racing for a different reason. "Mates are for life and I can't wait to spend mine with you."

She couldn't help herself, she leaned in and kissed him for all she was worth. She couldn't believe how lucky she was to be mated to someone who accepted her for who she was, even though they were a different species, and their families were mortal enemies. None of that mattered to Ramon, just as it didn't matter to her.

The sound of the elevator coming to life made them jump apart. Ramon muttered a few words in Spanish and scrubbed a hand over the stubble on his jaw.

"I don't want to get you in trouble with Mason," he said. "He's pretty angry and I'd hate for him to take that anger out on you."

"I can take care of myself. But thanks for thinking of me."

Yes, she was incredibly lucky. What if her mate had turned out to be someone as prejudiced as her brother? She didn't think she would have been able to stand being with a man like that, mates or not. Fortunately, it wasn't something she needed to worry about.

"Can you meet me tomorrow night?" Ramon asked quickly.

"Yes, of course."

"Do you know Puccini's restaurant?"

"I do." It was in a neutral part of the city that neither her family nor the Miguels could count as part of their territory.

"Great. Meet me outside at seven."

Saffy had just enough time to nod her agreement before the elevator doors dinged open and Mason stepped out, looking angrier than she had ever seen him.

"What the hell are you doing with my sister?" Mason all but growled.

Ramon raised his hands in front of him. "Just telling her you'd be out in a moment and that no charges were being brought against you."

"I should think not," Mason bit out. "You were the one trespassing on my property."

Saffy had a mind to tell him that the property actually belonged to their parents, but she thought it best not to antagonize him. "You ready to go?" she asked instead.

He grunted a reply, then followed her to the car. After she'd beeped the locks open and Mason had climbed in, she tossed Ramon a smile and wave before climbing into the car beside him. Mason didn't speak until they were back out on street level. He stiffened, then leaned in closer to her and inhaled deeply through his nose.

"Did that fucker lay a finger on you?"

She tried to hide her panic then looked across at him and frowned. "What?"

"Did he hit you—grab you, push you, anything?"

"No! Of course not. Why?"

"I can smell him on you," he said, his mouth twisted into an ugly sneer. "The stench of him makes me wanna heave."

She rolled her eyes. "You're imagining it."

"I'm gonna get him back for tonight," he said. "If it's the last thing I do."

She sighed heavily. "Mason."

"You don't think I'm going to let him get away with ruining Charlotte's party, do you? Those fucking Miguels have got a lot to answer for, but they'll get what's coming to them, you just wait and see."

Saffy had never been able to talk any sense into her brother and she wasn't sure what made her think that she might be able to this time, either. Regardless, she spent the rest of the drive home trying to dissuade him from whatever stupid revenge fantasy he'd already dreamed up. As per usual, Mason acted like he didn't hear a single word she said, but for once, his recklessness wasn't her top priority.

Chapter Five

Ramon

When Saffy got out of the cab and strolled along the sidewalk toward him, Ramon almost swallowed his tongue. She was wearing a skintight red dress cut high on her thigh and vampy red lipstick to match. If she had passed Ramon on the street, he would have been tempted to wolf whistle, even though he'd been raised better than that. But the fact that this was his mate made him glow with pride. She was a knockout. He couldn't believe that she was *his* mate.

"You look sensational," he greeted her when she reached him.

Ramon leaned in to give her a peck on the lips that sent his pulse soaring.

"Thanks," she said as they pulled apart. "You clean up nice yourself."

He beamed at her. "Thanks."

He wasn't wearing anything special, just jeans and a shirt, but he'd forgone his usual faded blue jeans for a pair of black ones and had changed his shirt five times before deciding on an olive-green one someone had one said went well with his complexion.

"You ready to eat?" he asked.

Saffy nodded to the restaurant. "Did you make a reservation?"

"No," he said with a frown. "They've usually got a table or two left empty. Why, do you think I should have?"

"Do you live alone?" she asked.

He grinned. "Yes. And you'd be more than welcome to come to my place, but I wouldn't be able to cook for you. I'm, uh, I'm a little behind on my grocery shopping this week."

She raised a perfectly sculpted brow. "You cook?"

"My mama raised me well."

"I can see that." She shrugged. "I'm not fussy what I eat, though. Pizza would be good, and it would be nice to have some time alone to talk."

"My place it is then." He offered her his arm and she took it without hesitation.

"You're not worried about being alone with me?"

She let out a very unladylike snort that Ramon couldn't help but find endearing.

"Please," she said with a wave of her hand. "I eat little bitty birdies like you for breakfast."

Ramon threw his head back and laughed. "*Really*? We're doing the cat and bird jokes already?"

She giggled. "I thought I'd sneak one in there, beat you to it."

"Smart move."

Their easy banter continued during the drive to Ramon's house and there were no gaps in the conversation. It was as if they'd known each other their entire lives, instead of only meeting for the first time the night before. It was the mate bond at work. It had to be. Ramon had known lots of newly mated couples of course, so he'd known what to expect, but knowing it and experiencing it firsthand were two different things entirely. Words would never have been able to explain how intense the feeling of being complete was, just from being in her presence.

After Ramon had let them into his house, he gave Saffy a quick tour of the place.

"It's a beautiful house," she said.

"Where do you live?" he asked.

She raised her brow and flashed her teeth in a grin. "You were there last night. I'm a lion shifter, remember?"

"Right, how could I forget?"

Most of the big cat species were solitary creatures so shifters, much like their animal counterparts, moved out of the family home as soon as humanly possible. Hawks were pretty much the same way. Ramon hadn't been able to wait to get a place of his own. But lions were different. In the wild, lion prides lived together in big familial groups and lion shifters were the same. It was extremely rare to find an unmated lion shifter living alone unless they'd been expelled from the pride and were forced to leave their parent's house.

"Must be hell on the dating life," Ramon remarked, then regretted it almost immediately. "Uh, never mind, don't answer that."

He didn't want to think about his mate's dating life before she met him. All shifter species, even hawks, were incredibly territorial and could be overly possessive. His bird was already ruffling its feathers at the thought of their mate with another man, and he wasn't doing much better. Of course she'd had relationships before she met him. That was normal. He just preferred not to think about it.

Saffy smiled. "Aww, look at you all jealous. It's cute."

"*Cute?*" he spluttered.

At six foot four, cute was not an adjective that was normally applied to him. The muscle and the SWAT weaponry helped with that.

Saffy grinned. "Would you have preferred strong, sexy, and manly?"

"Most definitely."

He flexed a bicep and cut her a wink, and was rewarded with a giggle.

"You're those things, too," she said, giving him a full body scan.

"Are you checking me out?"

"Yes."

"And?" he prompted shamelessly. "Do you like what you see?"

"What do you think?"

"I think," he said, his voice dropping an octave, "I'd like to hear you say it."

"There's nothing about you I don't like," she purred, her voice barely more than a whisper.

Her gaze met his and Ramon caught the heat in her eyes. The smile left his lips, and his pants felt a little bit tighter around the groin area. He thought he should ask if she was ready to order pizza because he wanted to make sure that he looked after his mate properly and that included making sure she ate well, but the look in her eyes told him she was hungry for something other than food.

He reached for her and was only truly satisfied that they were on the same page the moment his lips touched hers. A groan tore from her and she wrapped her arms around his neck, kissing him with a hunger that bordered on insatiable. He felt exactly the same way.

The attraction that simmered between them ignited into a passion that would have rivalled the hottest fire and it only burned brighter and more intensely the longer they kissed.

Ramon's tongue slid along Saffy's in an erotic dance, and she moaned, the sound going straight to his groin, hardening him almost to the point of pain. He ached for relief and could have wept in thanks when she reached between them and pressed the heel of her hand against his erection.

"Oh, Dios Mio," he breathed.

There was no time for a slow seduction, that would have to wait until the next time they were together. He needed her, now. Their lovemaking was going to be hot and heavy and incredibly fast. If there had been any doubt in his mind about that fact, it disappeared the moment Saffy backed him towards the couch, then, when the backs of his legs hit it and he sank down on the cushions, she straddled him, kissing him harder and deeper than before.

Ramon ran his hands up Saffy's smooth thighs until he reached the hem of her dress. He began to inch it higher, his hungry hands seemingly eager to touch every inch of bare flesh he encountered, but evidently, he wasn't moving fast enough for Saffy. She lifted her ass so that he could pull it all the way up to her waist. Then she started in on his belt, getting it undone in a flash before starting in on the button and zipper of his jeans. Before his brain could catch up with what his eyes were seeing, Saffy had her hands wrapped around his dick, her thumb sliding over the slit.

He threw his head back and groaned, wondering how long he could last while she touched him like that—hopefully long enough to get inside her, but the way this was going, he wasn't so sure. He forced himself to try to relax and calm down, but his damn stupid body didn't listen.

He opened his eyes then reached for the top of Saffy's strappy dress, pulling it down to expose her naked breasts. He leaned forward then took one of her nipples into his mouth. Maybe if he focused on her for a while, she'd be so distracted, she would leave him alone, so he'd have a few moments to calm down and get ahold of himself. Figuratively, not literally.

He wrapped his lips around her nipple, sucking on it gently then rolled it between his teeth. She cried out, her head falling back on her shoulders.

"Ramon," she breathed.

Damn, he liked it when she said his name all breathy like that. It made him even harder, if that was possible, and did nothing to aid his attempts not to completely lose control of himself before he'd had a chance to pleasure her. *Focus, Ramon,* he ordered himself. Trouble was, he already *was* focusing—on how damn hot his mate was. He flicked her nipple with his tongue then moved back and blew on it, enjoying the way it hardened into a tight little nub.

"Yes," she moaned.

He moved over to her other breast, but instead of tilting her head back again, she leaned forward, placing her arms on the couch on either side of him, caging him in, and then she began to move, gyrating her hips in a slow, sensual way, almost as if she was giving him a lap dance. And he loved every second of it. She moved her hips faster, grinding herself against him then reached for him again and it was Ramon's head that fell backwards. She used the position to her advantage to kiss her way up his neck before finding his mouth once again.

As the kiss grew deeper, the sexual tension between them increased until Ramon thought he was going to explode right that damn minute if he didn't get inside her. He was just about to take hold of her tiny waist to flip her over onto her back when Saffy rose up on her knees then reached between them and positioned him at her entrance. Then, without any further warning she sank down on his length, not stopping until he was seated as deep as her body would allow. A surprised grunt fell from his lips and a low, deep moan slid from hers.

Ramon thought she might have taken a moment to adjust to his considerable girth or rocked her hips slowly and gently until she had become accustomed to the stretch. She did none of that. Instead, she lifted her hips, rising up on his length until only the tip of him remained inside her then she sank down quickly again, taking him deep.

After that, she rode him hard and fast, her moans of pleasure turning into gasps as she clung to his shoulders, her fingers biting into his shoulder blades. Part of him wished she would extend her claws and mark him so that he'd have something visible on his body to remind himself of her when he looked in the mirror, even if the mark only lasted a day or two before it healed. The other part of him was determined to imprint every second of their lovemaking in his mind, so that even when they were apart, she would still be with him.

Spurred on by the noises she was making, Ramon snapped his hips up, meeting her thrust for thrust.

Soon, however, his shifter instincts took over, his need to dominate rising quickly to the surface and he was unable to ignore them for very long. He grabbed her around the waist, holding on tight then lifted her and flipped her over onto her back on the couch. Saffy squealed in delight as he came down on top of her and cried out as he thrust himself back inside her in one long, fluid motion. Now that he was the one on top, he was able to set the pace, but the time for going slow and steady had long since passed. All he had in him was fast and rough and raw. So that was what he gave her. To his relief and sheer delight, she took it all and begged him for more.

All too soon, Ramon felt the telltale sign of his impending release, but before he had to worry about slowing down or thinking unsexy thoughts to stave off his orgasm, Saffy gasped.

"I'm going to come!"

A moment later, she threw her head back and came hard, her soaking wet core constricting around him so much, he had no choice but to follow her over the edge. As his orgasm hit with tremendous force, he roared out his pleasure, his hips snapping before finally stilling as he spilled himself deep inside her.

After he'd stopped shaking from the aftershocks, he looked down into Saffy's beautiful pale blue eyes.

"Wow," she whispered. "That was…"

"Yeah," he agreed. "It was."

He leaned down and pressed his lips against his mate's then before he could move, his cellphone started to ring. With a soft groan, he groped into the back pocket of his jeans before sitting up and answering the call.

"Hello?"

His sister's panicked voice flooded down the line in a rapid-fire mix of English and Spanish that he wouldn't have been able to follow even if he wasn't inches from his naked mate.

"Maria? Maria, calm down," he said. "Tell me what's wrong."

He listened intently, his face twisting into a grimace the more he heard. "Hang tight, I'm on my way over. Call the police," he said.

He ended the call and sprang to his feet, doing up his jeans and then pausing to shoot a tormented look at his beautiful mate.

"Did you hear any of that?"

Saffy shook her head. "Couldn't really make out much. Was the woman crying?"

"Yeah," Ramon said. "It was Maria, my sister. She's pretty upset. She said someone just threw a brick through the window of her store. I should go… but…"

"But what?" She shook her head and gave him a shove. "Of course you should go. I'm not going to vanish in a sulk. Your sister needs you."

Ramon dipped his chin in relief and pulled on his shirt.

"Did she see anyone?" Saffy asked.

Ramon shook his head and grimaced. "No. But she said when she got outside, she could smell a male cat shifter."

Saffy closed her eyes and massaged her temple. "It was my damn brother, wasn't it?"

Ramon sighed. "Well, we don't know that for sure…"

"We know," she said. "Jesus Christ. When is my brother going to grow the hell up? It's not only the cost of the damage, but someone could have been hurt." Her eyes snapped up to meet Ramon's. "No one *was* hurt, were they?"

"No. But Maria said there was a human woman in the store at the time with her young son. The brick landed right at his feet."

Saffy retrieved her purse then pulled out her cellphone.

"Who are you calling?" Ramon asked.

"A cab. I'm gonna head home to see what my brother has to say about this. He's taken his stupid vendetta too far this time and hopefully, my father will agree with me."

Ramon wished he could be a fly on the wall for that conversation.

"Program my number into your phone and give me a call when you're done. I want to make sure you're okay."

"My brother might be a jackass, but he wouldn't hurt me," Saffy said.

"Maybe not, but just humor me, okay? Please?"

"Give me your number," she said.

Ramon breathed a sigh of relief and gave her his number. No-one had warned him having a mate would mean being in a constant state of panic.

Chapter Six

Saffy

Saffy let herself into the house and strode into the living room to find her brother lounged out in front of the television, nursing a beer. It was highly unusual to see him at home this early on a Friday night, instead of out drinking and causing trouble with Leon and Jason, and that in and of itself was suspicious. She threw her purse down onto the coffee table and glanced at the TV.

"You stay in tonight?" she asked nonchalantly.

"Nah, I just got home," Mason said.

Bingo.

She turned to face her brother. She'd never really gotten along with him. They'd argued when they were young, like all kids, but it had only gotten worse as they got older. The whole pride seemed oblivious to it, but it was like he'd never grown up. He refused to take any of his responsibilities seriously, and he always took advantage of their parents, leveraging his role in the pride and as their eldest son to get whatever he wanted. The thought of him one day leading the pride would be laughable, if it wasn't so terrifying. And that wasn't even taking into consideration the way he treated people.

But tonight, he'd reached an all-time low. Although for all she knew, he could have been doing things like this all the time, and this was the first time she'd found out about it. The thought was a depressing one. Just how many people had he terrorized over the years? One, two, dozens—more?

She turned to face him. "Did you throw a brick through the window of Maria Miguel's store just now?"

Mason paused with the beer bottle halfway to his mouth. "How do you know about that?"

Maria sucked in an angry breath. "You are some piece of work, you know that? What the hell is wrong with you, Mason?"

"Those fucking Miguels had it coming," he spat.

"Did you know there was a human in the store with a young child? Your brick nearly hit him. But that's entirely beside the point. What you did was wrong."

Mason jumped to his feet. "You didn't answer me, *sis*. How do you know all that?"

She glared at him.

"Are you screwing that *wetback*?" he shouted at her.

Saffy saw red. She drew her arm back then slapped him across the face so hard the palm of her hand smarted and Mason stumbled, the beer in his bottle sloshing over his fingers.

"Don't you dare call him that!" she shouted back at him. "He's worth ten of you."

"What the hell is going on in here?" their father asked, striding into the room and staring at each of them in turn.

"She's fucking Miguel," Mason spat.

Her father froze, standing stock still for a moment before he turned to her, his lip curled in distaste.

"Is that true?" he asked, his voice as cold as ice.

Saffy opened her mouth to reply, but when she didn't answer her father quickly enough, anger crept into every line on his face.

"Is it goddamn *true*?" he shouted. "Are you seeing the hawk shifter?"

"He's my mate!" she shouted back.

She waited for more shouting. None came.

Saffy had seen her brother and father angry before. But this was something else. Something that scared her. Rage poured out of her brother in waves.

"It's not true," Mason said. "It can't be."

"You're to stop seeing him," her father commanded. "Immediately."

She looked at each of them in turn, her mouth popping open in disbelief. She zeroed in on her father.

"He's my mate. You can't forbid me to see him." It was physically painful to imagine not seeing him again. She shook her head. "You just…can't."

"I can," her father said coldly, "and I have. I am your dominant. Disobey me, and you will not only be thrown out of this house, you will no longer have a place in this pride."

"Then I guess there's nothing left to say."

She grabbed her purse from the coffee table then turned and walked out of the living room and then right out of the house. Outside, she retrieved her cellphone then dialed Ramon's number.

"Saffy?" he answered. "What happened? Are you okay?"

"They know," she said, as she crossed the front lawn, fighting the urge to look back over her shoulder. Were they watching from the windows? She drew in a shaking breath. "I had to tell them. And my father… well, let's just say he didn't take it well. At all."

"Hang tight," Ramon said. "I'll be there in ten. You're moving in with me."

She closed her eyes and breathed a sigh of relief. He'd said it without even hesitating, as though it was the most obvious thing in the world that he would take her in. As if it was perfectly normal to move in with someone a day after you'd met them. It wasn't, of course, not even in shifter circles between soul mates, but that didn't seem to bother Ramon in the slightest and if she was being honest, it didn't bother her, either. A fated mate was pretty much a done deal, anyway, right? Hearts and flowers, and true love…the stuff of fairy tales. Something she'd spent her whole life alternately dreading and wishing for.

Sure, it would have been nice to spend some more time getting to know Ramon before she moved in with him, but this just felt…right.

She was only sorry that her family couldn't accept Ramon as easily and whole-heartedly as she could.

Chapter Seven

Ramon

"You sure you're ready for this?" Ramon asked as he stood completely naked in front of his mate.

Her gaze roamed salaciously over his body, and he couldn't help standing a little straighter and puffing out his chest. Inside, his bird preened under her attention.

"Sounds to me like you're stalling," Saffy said, a coy smile playing across her full lips. "I can go first if you're afraid."

His inner bird bristled at that and even the playful raise of his mate's eyebrows, and the curve of her luscious mouth couldn't convince it that she was only teasing.

Mate challenges us. Shift. Show her our regal plumage. Show her our majesty. Shift.

Ramon grinned. "All right, you asked for it."

He crouched down then let the change rush over his body. When it came on, it came on fast. At first, it felt like an itch over his skin, like thousands of ants were crawling over it. Then the sensation morphed into something that wasn't entirely uncomfortable, but strange nonetheless. Or had been, back when he was a kid learning to shift. He wasn't a kid now. He was an adult, a member of a SWAT team. So why the heck was he so terrified?

Mate will like what she sees, his bird squawked. *How could she not?*

If his head hadn't been otherwise engaged changing size and shape, he'd have shaken it at his animal's irrepressible vanity. Sometimes, it was more like a peacock than a hawk.

His feathers began to grow out and he felt the need to have an all over body shake the way a dog did when it was wet. Lastly came the most magical part of his shift when he let his bird out fully, and his human form began to fade away. His bird was always elated to break free from its confinement so that it could get up into the air and soar. Ramon looked forward to that part too, but today wasn't about letting his bird out to fly, it was about letting his bird meet Saffy, and her lion.

Of course, cats and birds were mortal enemies, but a shifter's other half usually recognized their mate after the disorienting sensation of the shift had worn off. Ramon was hoping his bird would recognize Saffy's lion as his mate, too. Usually, like most adult shifters, he had full control of his animal when he shifted. But around Saffy, it seemed like all bets were off. About everything.

He had brought her to a small reserve that he knew to be quiet at that time of the evening. People probably wouldn't have freaked out if they saw a hawk somewhere near them, but a lion was a different matter entirely. Saffy's pride had a large nature reserve where they all went to shift, but with the way she had left things with her family, it wouldn't have been good for her to go there. And it *definitely* wouldn't have been advisable for her to take a hawk shifter with her on pride territory, mate or not.

Almost at once, Ramon felt his bird vying for control, for the chance to sweep and glide through the air, wowing their mate with their aerial grace. A loud screech burst from their throat, and his wings flapped wildly. The bird had just bent its head to start cleaning his already immaculate feathers then stopped abruptly when he heard the sharp intake of breath.

"You're beautiful," Saffy said in a reverent whisper.

Ramon took advantage of his animal's awed distraction to wrest back control and then preened, hoping she hadn't noticed his embarrassing slip. It had been over a decade since his bird had taken over like that, and it had earned him a bad enough ribbing then.

Content his bird was back under control, and thrilled that Saffy seemed to find his bird form so pleasing, he hopped around in a circle—the closest he could come to a twirl—and was rewarded with her amused chuckle. He bobbed his head, and then stretched out his wings…because when it came down to it, size really did matter. And his wings were huge.

She grinned. "Wow, look how big and powerful you are."

Mate likes us, the bird said to him, with an unmistakable note of smugness. He would have grinned, if beaks had been cut out for grinning, at the bird's reaction. Of course she likes us, you idiot, he thought back at the bird. She's our mate. And yet, he couldn't help but share the animal's jubilation. The lioness was awed by the hawk.

She stretched out a hand and ran her fingertips across his feathers in a gentle caress. He closed his eyes at the glorious sensation, thrumming in his throat with utter contentment. He was fairly certain he was in hawk heaven.

After a while, she got to her knees and asked, "Are you ready to meet my cat?"

Ramon's inner bird flapped its wings in agitation, but he kept his physical form completely still. He was fully in control, and he would need to be. If Saffy had a lapse in control over her cat the way he had when he'd first shifted, then natural instincts could kick in. He loved his mate, and would never allow any harm to come to her. He just couldn't be certain her inner cat felt the same way about his bird.

But he would keep them both safe. He nodded his head a few times to convey that he was ready, and she let out a nervous giggle that he thought might have been the most beautiful sound ever uttered in this meadow.

"All right then, let's do this."

He watched in rapt fascination as the air shimmered around his mate's body and fur began to sprout from her arms. His bird didn't like that bit as much, but he was rapt. Then her body began to change into her cat, her shapely figure becoming larger and yet still lithe, with effortless grace. He hopped back a couple of feet to give her more room and to put a safe distance between them in case the cat's instincts triggered during the shift.

When his mate had completed her shift, all he could do was stare at her in awe. Saffy's lion was *huge*—the biggest he'd ever seen up close. She stretched lazily then licked her giant paws before lifting her head and locking him in place with what could only have been described as a death glare.

His bird urged him to take flight, to flee, but instead, he stayed perfectly still. It's okay, he reassured the animal. She's our mate. She won't harm us. Still, he kept his eyes trained on her as she got up on those giant paws and inched closer to him. She stopped a few feet away and her nose twitched, then she fell on her side and her chest started to emit a weird rumbling noise that might have been the best sound he had ever heard in his life. Bar none. It was hypnotic and it made his legs hop closer as if they had a mind of their own. He was so close now, she could have reached out and grabbed him, but he was entranced by the rumbling noise and had to get closer to it. Much closer. He cocked his head to the side, the better to hear it.

Quicker than he would have imagined possible, Saffy leapt to her feet then headbutted him with her massive skull. He bounced back a few steps and blinked as she took off at a full out gallop across the meadow. He let out a strangled squawk in surprise and amusement, and then flapped his massive wings. It was like that, was it? Fine. It was *on*.

He took off after her, soaring over the meadow and chased her around and around until darkness started to fall. Eventually they both got tired, and collapsed next to one another on the warm evening grass.

Chapter Eight

Saffy

"Are you sure you're okay to walk in those heels?" Ramon asked as he slammed his car door shut then bleeped on the locks.

She grinned. "I could run in these heels. I've practically lived in heels like this for the past decade."

His eyes widened then he shook his head, grinning wryly. "The things women do in the name of fashion."

"Oh, come on," she said. "I'm meeting all your SWAT team mates and their mates tonight, would you have been happy for me to turn up in sneakers?"

"Only two of the guys have mates," he said with a shrug. "And actually, I wouldn't have minded. You look beautiful whatever you wear."

"Good answer."

"I thought so."

She chuckled as she took his extended arm and let him lead her along the street to the party. Saffy hadn't told Ramon, but she was really excited to meet his friends. It was just another step in cementing their relationship as mates. Everything had been going really well between them, but meeting the friends was a big step in any relationship. And his SWAT team were like his second family. She felt a flutter of excitement about meeting them…and more than a small amount of trepidation. What if they didn't like her? There was no worry about the reverse, of course—Ramon had nothing but good things to say about his teammates and she trusted his judgement. If he liked them, she had no doubt that she would, too.

They chatted amiably as they walked along then Ramon led her up the path of a modest house that was small, but well maintained.

"Oh wow, what is that smell?" Saffy asked as they walked up the path to the front door.

Ramon grinned. "Honeyed buns and cinnamon rolls if I'm not mistaken," he said. "Maya owns a bakery, so she probably catered most of her engagement party herself. Well, it's not an actual engagement party, just a small get together for the team."

The panic that had threatened to overtake her subsided enough for her to smile. Thank God it was just the team, because heels or no, she was most definitely *not* dressed for an engagement party.

"A bakery, huh? Nice."

Ramon nodded. "Gray is always bringing baked goods into work."

"Gray?" Saffy asked.

She still hadn't got to grips with the names of all his teammates, not helped by the fact that Ramon seemed to use their first names and their team names interchangeably, but she hoped that putting faces to the pairs of names would help.

Ramon nodded. "His real name is Cole, but Gray is his SWAT team nickname. Gray wolf shifter," he explained.

"Ah, got it. So let me see if I got this right. There's Gray, Ted, Ice, Kit…"

"Flint, and yours truly," Ramon finished for her.

"How come your nickname is the only one that's your actual shifter species?"

Ramon grinned. "Probably because hawks are the shit so nothing else was required."

Saffy threw her head back and laughed. "Right, got it."

Ramon knocked on the front door and it was opened a moment later by a huge shifter whose face broke out into a grin as soon as his eyes set on Ramon.

"Hawk," he greeted him warmly. "Come on in."

"Not too early, are we?"

"Not at all, you're right on time."

"This is my mate, Saffy," Ramon introduced her, with a smile so wide it almost split his face in half. "Saffy, this is my teammate and friend, Gray."

He reached out a giant hand and shook hers. "Hey. You can call me Cole."

Music and excited chatter greeted them as soon as they stepped foot into the living room. On one side of the room, three gigantic men stood, taking pulls from their beer bottles and shooting the breeze, and on the other side were three women, two of whom were chatting excitedly amongst themselves. The other woman looked as if she would prefer to be standing with the men. One of the women was heavily pregnant and she was the one who was happily showing the other two her engagement ring.

"Let me introduce you to everyone," Ramon said.

"Okay, great."

He took her over to meet the men first. "Okay so you just met Gray. Firstly, the mammoth of a man is Flint."

Saffy scented the air then frowned. Was he a… No, she must have been mistaken. He couldn't have been. The last she'd heard, that species was extinct.

"Ted you might remember from your sister's party the other night," Ramon said. Nash dipped his chin in greeting. "And that's Ice."

"I'm the handsome one of the bunch," Ice said with a grin that managed to be both boyish and downright dirty at the same time. A blush stole over her cheeks and she fought the urge to fan them. Fortunately, Ramon didn't notice it.

"Everyone, this is my mate, Saffy."

After they had all said hello, and Saffy and Ramon had talked to them for a little while, he took her arm and guided her over to the women.

"This is my mate," he said to them all. "Saffy, this is Kit, Aria, and Maya."

"Hi," Saffy greeted them warmly.

The pregnant woman rushed forward and embraced her. "Cole told me you're a lion shifter, is that right?"

Saffy nodded, grinning at the look of awe on Maya's face. "I sure am."

"Wow," Aria said. "Are you as big as a real lion?"

"Um, probably bigger."

"Wow," her and Maya said in unison.

"Oh, congratulations on the engagement," Saffy said. "And on the baby."

"Thanks!"

Saffy turned to the other woman. "Kit, right?"

She nodded. "Good to meet you."

"You, too. Ramon says you're the only woman on the team."

Kit grinned. "Someone's got to keep all those big macho dudes in check."

Saffy laughed. "I don't doubt you could do it, either. Ramon says you're a panther shifter, right?" She frowned. "I don't get it, though. *Kit?*"

The tall, muscular woman rolled her eyes. "That was the guys' idea of a joke when I joined the team. It's short for *kitty kat*." Another eye roll. "Sometimes with those boys, you've just got to pick your battles. I was exasperated at first, but now, it's kinda grown on me."

"Well, I'm glad someone's around to keep them in line." She glanced across the room where the guys were laughing and shoving each other around. "Though it seems like that job might be akin to herding cats."

Kit snorted with laughter. "You got that right."

"Wow. Oh! Where are my manners? Let me get you a drink!" Maya said. "Sorry, I haven't been drinking you know, since the pregnancy and I keep forgetting other people don't have my restriction. And now, apparently, that they need a drink at all. I'm blaming baby brain. Sorry," she said again. "I'm a terrible host."

Saffy shrugged. "Don't worry about it."

"Um, we've got beer, wine, or you can have a cocktail," she said.

"Oh, a cocktail sounds great," Saffy said before she noticed Aria and Kit vigorously shaking their heads. Too late.

"Great!" Maya said and she dashed off to make the drink.

Saffy leaned in. "What's wrong with the cocktails?"

Kit chuckled wickedly. "You'll see."

A few moments' later, Maya had returned with Saffy's drink. After the matching expressions of horror on Aria and Kit's face, Saffy put the drink to her mouth and took a sip. And immediately began coughing.

Aria turned away to face the wall as Kit slapped Saffy on the back.

"Must have gone down the wrong hole," Saffy said after the coughing fit had subsided.

Her eyes started to water.

"Kit, Aria, do you want another cocktail?"

"I'll take a beer," they said at the same time. Saffy wondered if it was too late to swap her drink, too.

After Maya had gone off to grab their beers, Saffy leaned in closer to their little huddle. "Wow. Did she forget the soda?"

Aria's shoulders shook as she laughed. "Strong, right?"

"I'll say. If I get through all of this, Ramon is going to have to carry me out of here." And then she shrugged. "Oh well. At least I'm not an angry drunk."

"Weepy?" Aria suggested.

Saffy shook her head then leaned in again and whispered, "Horny."

They seemed to find this hilarious, and threw their heads back laughing hysterically. Saffy decided to blame it on the vodka.

"So, how much did Hawk tell you about us?" Maya asked when she got back with the two beers.

"Nothing at all," Saffy said and then narrowed her eyes. "Why, is there a juicy story in there somewhere?"

All three sets of eyes widened, and they proceeded to tell her their stories. It turned out Maya's brother was pretty much a petty criminal who had decided kidnap was a good way to earn money and he'd ended up arrested by Ramon's SWAT team. It was how her and Gray had met. That might have been a niceish story apart from the bit where she was almost killed by bad guys. Her brother sounded a lot like Saffy's brother. Sure, Mason hadn't lowered himself to kidnapping yet, but there was always time. Then again, maybe she was doing Maya's brother an injustice—he at least seemed to have seen the error of his ways. Saffy suspected she'd be waiting a long time for Mason to have a similar awakening.

Aria's story was even more surprising. Aria worked in Maya's bakery and that was how they knew each other and how she came to meet her mate, Nash who was Gray's friend and teammate. But before that, she'd been married—there was a whole crazy tale of which being kidnapped by bad guys seemed to be the least scary part.

Saffy couldn't believe what she was hearing. She was starting to suspect hanging out with these guys led to trouble. Good thing she was a lion shifter, and plenty capable of taking care of herself.

"So, what's your story, Saffy?" Aria asked.

Saffy shrugged. "Not much to tell really. It kinda pales in comparison to yours."

She told them how her family and Ramon's had been involved in a feud for years and how her family wouldn't accept Ramon as her mate. The more she talked, the more she took sips from her drink, and it wasn't until she reached the part about being kicked out of the pride that she realized she'd drained the whole thing.

"I'll get you a refill," Maya said.

Saffy was so worked up by telling them about how her family wouldn't accept her mate, she forgot to refuse the second drink.

By the time Ramon strolled over to her a couple of hours later and lazily wrapped his arm around her shoulder, she was on drink number three, which put her somewhere in the danger zone between drunk off her ass and sick as a dog.

"Hey baby, you having fun?" he asked.

She squinted at him. "Did I tell you how handsome I think you are?"

Ramon chuckled quietly. "You did, but it's always nice to hear."

"I think you're handsome," she said.

He shook his head. "I think someone might be a little bit drunk."

"Really?" she said, turning to look over her shoulder. "Who?"

All three women and Ramon shared a laugh, Ramon laughing a little bit too hard.

"And on that note," he said. "Maya, thank you for your hospitality, but I think I should get this one home."

"My pleasure," she said. "And thank you for the card and the gift certificate. Little one will appreciate them."

"You're welcome."

Ramon tried to lead her to the door, but Saffy insisted on personally saying goodbye to everyone in the room. By the end of it, Ramon had to practically drag her away from the party.

"Saffy!" Aria shouted after them. "Don't forget, you're not an angry drunk."

"What was that all about?" Ramon asked as they were walking back to the car.

"I can't imagine," she said, but then she burst out laughing and nearly toppled over on her heels.

If Ramon hadn't been supporting her weight, she would have face planted on the sidewalk.

He shook his head and let out a throaty sounding chuckle. "Can't imagine my ass," he said under his breath. "You are so full of shit."

For some reason, this made her laugh even harder. But hey, at least she wasn't an angry drunk. And her mate was very, *very* handsome.

Chapter Nine

Ramon

Ramon tried to focus and prepare himself mentally for what they were about to face as they rode in the vehicle on the way to their latest assignment—an active shooter who had barricaded himself in a classroom at an elementary school. They didn't know if the shooter had any ammunition left and so far, there were no reports that he'd shot any of the pupils or teachers, but they couldn't afford to take any chances. They had to assume he was still armed and very, very dangerous. It was a situation that, despite all of their training, every one of them dreaded.

Ramon tugged at the neck of his shirt. It was sweltering hot in the back of the vehicle. It didn't help that he was sat next to Flint. The man was like his own personal furnace. Ramon wouldn't have been surprised if he walked away with a suntan.

"How are things going with Saffy?" Nash asked

"Good," Ramon replied. "Great, actually. The past couple of days have been amazing, but I know she misses her family. She tried calling her mom last night, but she hung up on her. I mean, what kind of woman does that to her own daughter?"

"Perhaps it was her father's influence?" Nash suggested.

"Yeah, that's what Saffy seems to think, but even so. It's her mom. I know it's got to be difficult to go against your mate's wishes, but, what, she couldn't even stand up to him for her own child who hasn't done anything wrong? It sucks. I feel for her, I really do."

"You don't think there's any reasoning with her father?"

"I doubt it. On the few occasions that I had dealings with him he seemed stubborn and unwilling to listen to anyone else's point of view."

"He thinks he knows it all then, eh?"

Ramon snorted. "Pretty much, yeah. Cat shifters, right?"

"Hey!" Kit objected. "I heard that."

Nash snorted and Ramon grinned, but when his cellphone started ringing, it changed to a frown. Only a handful of people had the number. It was for emergencies only. His team were allowed to take their cellphones out into the field, but they were only supposed to use them for work related issues or emergencies. He pulled the phone out of his pocket then glanced at the display.

"It's my mate," he said to the car at large.

He pressed a button then lifted the cell to his ear. "Hey babe, everything okay?"

"Ramon?" Saffy said, her voice tight and breathless.

Ramon sat up straighter in his seat. "What's wrong?"

"Mason is here with two of his friends," she said quickly. "They're drunk."

Ramon let out a stream of curse words in Spanish. "Are you still at work?"

"Yeah, my manager, Lorraine, told them they had to leave the salon and now they're out on the street shouting for me to come out." She dropped her voice and spoke rapidly. "I'm surprised they listened to Lorraine because she's human. Mason hasn't got much respect for humans."

Mason didn't have a lot of respect for anyone, Ramon thought but he kept it to himself. That wouldn't help her right now, and he *needed* to help her. He cursed under his breath.

"We've got an active shooter situation and he's in a school so it's pretty urgent."

"Oh, my God."

"Yeah. I can't leave right now." He raked a hand through his hair. "You know I'm the sharpshooter on the team, so they might need me."

"No, of course," she said. "I wouldn't expect you to leave something like that. I just, I didn't know what to do, that's why I called."

Fuck.

Ramon hated that he couldn't be there for his mate when she needed him. Mates came before all else, but they were talking about the protection of children. He couldn't walk away from something like that, no matter how much the shifter in him wanted to go charging to help his mate.

"Has he threatened you?" Ramon asked.

"No, not really. He's just been abusive."

Damn it. Happy as he was that Mason hadn't escalated as far as threatening, if he had threatened her then she could have call the police, but otherwise, there wasn't a lot they could do.

"If he does, I want you to call 911, okay? Whatever you do, don't go out there to talk to him. If he's drunk and with his friends, you don't know what he's capable of. Remember, he hates me, so right now he probably hates you by association. As soon as I'm done at the school, I'll come straight over."

"Okay, I'll let you get off. Talk to you soon."

"Bye, babe, and remember, if at any point you are afraid for your safety or the safety of anyone else in the salon, you phone the police, okay?"

"I don't think it will come to that. I'll speak to you soon. Love you."

She disconnected.

"Goddamn, fucking, shit!" Ramon exploded. "You guys hear all that?"

"Yeah," they all murmured in unison.

"That brother sounds like a piece of work," Flint said. "Look, I'm sorry. If we could spare you…"

"You don't even need to say it. I know how important this is. It just sucks that I can't be there for her. I've only been mated for a couple of days, and already I'm dropping the ball."

"You can't look at it that way," Gray said. "I'm sure your mate understands how important your job is."

"Yeah, doesn't help *her* though, does it?"

It wasn't even as if there was anyone that Ramon could call to go to her aid. He hadn't told his parents about the mating yet, but his father hated the Brown family so much, he suspected they would react in a similar way to how hers had. Not for the first time, he wished they could just put the past where it belonged and get along.

"We're here," Flint said. "In the zone, people. We do this one by the book, just like we planned. Room by room, floor by floor, slowly and methodically. Sorry, Hawk."

Ramon waved away the apology. He switched his cellphone to silent then a moment later they were all peeling out of the back of the vehicle with their weapons and jogging towards the barricade that had been set up by the local police. Local cops had been first on scene and immediately called for the FBI's assistance. Flint headed over to speak to the officer in charge while the rest of the team awaited instructions.

"She'll be all right, Hawk," Kit said as they waited for Flint.

When the team had to split up into pairs, Kit was Ramon's partner, so he'd spent more time with her than with any of the guys and as a result, was probably closer to her than anyone else on the team. He heaved a sigh.

"Yeah, but I should be there for her."

"It's not your fault. Besides, she's not some weak, helpless human. She's a *lion* shifter. They're strong and they can take care of themselves. And from what you've told me, and what I saw of her, she's not stupid or reckless, either. She's not gonna go outside and provoke her brother—she'll know better than that."

Ramon nodded, somewhat comforted by Kit's words. For the time being, he had to just trust that his mate would be okay until he could get there. And Kit was right: she was smart, and she was sensible, and he *did* trust her.

In his line of work, it was essential to keep focused on the job or people could get hurt. It wouldn't be the first time a member of the team had been hurt because another member had dropped the ball. They'd been lucky someone hadn't been killed that day, and that was the only reason they'd all walked away from it. If something like that was to happen again, the next person might not have the same luck. They were shifters, sure, who were stronger than humans and could heal much more quickly, but they weren't invincible. They bled, which meant they could bleed out.

He was damned if he was going to be responsible for a repeat of that day, especially when there were humans in the line of fire. They didn't have the same healing advantages as shifters.

When Flint came back to them, they huddled in to listen to what he had learned from the officer in charge of the scene.

"So, the police have been in contact with a teacher in the school who has her cellphone on her. She's barricaded herself in her classroom with her students."

Gray nodded his head in approval as Flint continued,

"Naturally, they're all scared stiff, but the school have protocols for shootings and the children have all been through the drills. Three teachers managed to get their students out, but there are two more teachers in there they haven't been able to make contact with, and they each have a class full of students."

Unease stirred in Ramon's gut. That was a lot of bodies. A lot of potential cannon fodder for the perp.

"The teacher they spoke to said she thought the gunman might be holding one of those classes hostage, because she saw him enter one of the rooms before she barricaded the door to her class."

Someone cussed, Ramon didn't see who, and Flint pressed on, his face impassive.

"It's a small school—a main entrance, a back entrance that leads out to a small recreation area, and a few fire exits. There's a teachers' lounge and a cafeteria, but that's about it. We'll split up and circle the building. Hawk, I don't have to tell you how important your skills could be on this job. In an ideal world, we don't want to be shooting anyone in front of children, but if it comes down to him or them, you take the shot."

Ramon nodded his agreement. "Understood."

"The shooter was last seen entering the third classroom on the left as you go in through the front entrance. We'll circle the building and use our shifter senses to try to locate the shooter and determine if he's alone or has hostages. This is strictly threat assessment unless the shooter emerges and we're able to apprehend him. Understood?"

He turned his steely gaze round the group and they all nodded their agreement. No-one wanted to risk a kid getting caught in the crossfire.

"It's worth mentioning that this is an active shooter, but as far as we're aware, he hasn't shot anyone in the school, he just ran in there to hide after discharging his weapon out on the street. Currently, there are no known fatalities or even injuries as a result of this man, but that doesn't mean there won't be. Anyone have any questions?"

When no one said anything, Flint nodded. "Okay. Let's move out. Hawk, you cover the front entrance. I'll cover the back. Kit and Ice, circle the right of the building and Gray and Ted, you go left. Let's do this."

They ran toward the school then quickly broke off into their assigned tasks. Ramon hated that he had nothing to do but stand sentry at the front of the school because it left him alone with his thoughts, but he understood the reason why. If the shooter tried to leave by any of the exits, they would run into either him or Flint. Ramon was the best shot on the team and Flint a very close second.

The front door to the school was closed. He peered through the glass, but there was no movement from within, so he pressed his ear to the door. As he didn't hear a peep, he opened the door as quietly and carefully as possible. Leading with his sniper rifle, he checked behind the door on either side then when he was sure it was clear, he left the door open, got down on one knee and trained his rifle straight ahead of him. He waited.

He was still in the same position twenty minutes later. He'd tried not to let his mind wander to what might be happening with his mate, but he couldn't stop his thoughts from straying to her every now and then. When Gray and Ted arrived back from their recon mission, they stopped about five feet away from Ramon and whispered their findings.

"Confirmed only one gunman," Ted said. "The teacher was partially right. He's in the third classroom on the left, but he's alone. It must have been one of the classrooms the teachers managed to evacuate. I heard him breathing in there, so I chanced a look through the window. He's sitting with his back against the door, rocking. He looks half crazed. His gun is in his lap—it looked like a standard issue Glock. I just told Flint, he wants to—"

Ted cut off the rest of his sentence when a classroom door opened and the shooter stepped out into the hallway, brandishing his gun.

"FBI! Drop your weapon!" Ramon shouted, causing the man to look up in alarm, his eyes wide with fear.

Evidently, he hadn't even realized they were there.

A moment of indecision crossed the man's face, but instead of throwing his gun on the floor, he lifted his arm to point it straight ahead of himself. Ramon didn't hesitate. He fired a shot from his rifle, hitting the man in the shoulder of the arm that held the gun.

The force of the shot sent him flying backward and he went down heavily on his ass, the gun skittering across the floor several feet away from him. Ramon jumped to his feet and hurried along the hallway, his weapon still trained forward.

"Stay on the ground!" he shouted.

The man was groaning in pain, holding his shoulder and rolling around on the floor. When Ramon approached, he kicked the man's gun further from his reach and kept his rifle trained on the man as Ted and Gray patted him down for any other weapons and came up empty. Once they were content he had nothing concealed, they cuffed his hands then hauled him to his feet and led him outside.

Flint, Ice, and Kit caught up to them moments later. Flint checked in with the officer in charge from the local PD, and sent Ted and Gray to take the perp to the station while the rest of the team headed back to headquarters to debrief. Ramon tried to call Saffy as soon as he cleared the school, but she didn't pick up the call. He tried her twice more on the way back to headquarters. Still no answer. It was pretty obvious she hadn't just missed his calls—one, he could believe, two, even. But three was a stretch. And if she wasn't picking up, there was a reason for it.

The unease prickling at the back of his neck had become full blown anxiety by the time he made it into the parking lot. He turned to Flint, but before he could say a word, the team leader beat him to it.

"Go. But you know the drill: you discharged your weapon and shot a suspect. I need that paperwork on my desk by first thing tomorrow."

"Thanks, Flint, you got it."

He switched cars and peeled out of the parking lot at breakneck speed and arrived at the salon where Saffy worked a short while later. There was no sign of Mason and his friends outside and the air didn't even carry a trace of their scent. Hoping that meant they'd given up and left his mate alone and that she was busy so hadn't been able to answer her phone, Ramon rushed inside, scanning the room. His heart sank, taking its false hope with it. Saffy was nowhere to be seen.

"Ramon?" a short, petite blonde woman asked as she approached him.

He nodded. "Yes, that's me. Where's Saffy?"

The woman shook her head. "Her brother and his friends came in here and she went with them."

Ramon stilled, his heart landing somewhere in the vicinity of his throat. "Excuse me?"

She nodded. "I asked her if she wanted me to call the police, but Mason started to get really angry. He was frightening the customers so Saffy told me not to bother and left with him."

When the woman took in the expression on Ramon's face, her eyes widened. "He's her brother. You don't think he'd hurt her, do you?"

Ramon would have answered but he was already halfway out the door. His stomach twisted painfully as he ran back to his car. He couldn't imagine where Mason would have taken her, but he headed for her parent's house, praying that her brother would be stupid enough to just take her home.

He parked outside their house, then jogged up to the front door and rang the doorbell. Too impatient to wait for a reply, he pounded on the door with his fists.

"Open up!" he shouted, his anxiety increasing with each passing second.

A few moments later, the door was pulled open and Saffy's father, Owen, stood between its jambs.

"What the hell are *you* doing here?" he bit out. "You've caused enough trouble for this family already, don't you think?"

"Are they here?" Ramon asked, trying to shoulder his way into the house.

The older man stood his ground. "Is *who* here?"

"Saffy!" Ramon shouted. "With Mason and his degenerate sidekicks."

"No, they are not here," Owen said. "Saffy is no longer welcome in my home."

"I don't believe you." When Ramon tried to shoulder past him again, the man let out a burst of alpha power so strong, it had Ramon rocking back on his heels.

"If you don't leave immediately, I will call the police to have you arrested for—"

"Phone them," Ramon said. "Go on. Do it. Perhaps you'll be able to explain to them why Mason kidnapped his sister from her place of work an hour ago."

The man scoffed. "*Kidnapped?* Why would Mason kidnap his own sister? You're delusional."

"She called me from work. Scared out of her mind. Mason and his friends were drunk. When I got there to pick her up, her boss said they came into the salon. Mason was angry and shouting, scaring the customers. He forced Saffy to go with them."

"I'm sure she's perfectly fine," he said coldly. "Mason would never hurt his sister."

"Are you willing to stake your life on that? Because if he harms one hair on her head, I'll hold you personally responsible. He hurts her, I swear to God, I will tear him apart, then I'll come for you."

"Are you *threatening* me?" Owen asked, incredulous.

"Yes," Ramon said. "You bet your ass I am."

Chapter Ten

Saffy

"You're never gonna see him again," Mason said. "*Ever.* Then you can come back home, and we'll pretend it never happened."

Saffy rolled her eyes. "Tell me, would *you* leave *your* mate on my say so?"

"He's not your fucking mate!" Mason roared in her face, his spittle hitting her in the cheek. His breath wreaked of alcohol, but he wasn't slurring his words, and he was steady on his feet. Overpowering him was out.

She'd tried to leave three times already, but each time Mason had grabbed her and pulled her back. The third time he'd shaken her hard enough to make her teeth rattle then slapped her across the face with enough force to split her lip. The wound had healed, but the deep-seated terror inside her had only spread.

Mason had never struck her before. He was a bastard, but he'd never been a woman beater. It just went to prove how much he hated Ramon, and how low he was willing to sink to get his own way.

She had tried to call her mate earlier, but Mason had grabbed the phone out of her hand and threw it across the room so hard it smashed against the wall, the back flying in one direction, the body of the phone in another. She glanced over at the shattered pieces. She was pretty sure that wouldn't be working again any time soon.

Mason went back to pacing the living room of his friend's house while he tried to 'talk some sense into her.' Mason had been drunk off his ass when he'd come to the salon earlier, but they'd started drinking again as soon as they arrived at Leon's house, knocking back whisky like it was going out of fashion. It was only his natural shifter tolerance to alcohol that was keeping him on his feet, more was the pity. If he'd just pass out drunk somewhere, she could slip out while he was snoring.

Saffy eyed the clock on the living room wall. Was it too much to hope that Leon's parents would get home from work soon, or anyone else who might talk some sense into him? Surely even he wasn't dumb enough to think that just because he was Mason's friend, he could get away with kidnapping the daughter of his dominant?

Like he was reading her mind, Leon leered down at her. "Don't worry, the rest of the family are in Fort Lauderdale. We won't be disturbed."

Her stomach rolled. So much for that. No-one was coming to her rescue.

With each new swig he took from the bottle, Mason got more and more het up. And Leon was alternating between tossing her glares of disgust and looking at her like she was something to eat. Jason, who was usually the most sensible out of the three, if such a thing was possible, looked just as angry and sickened by her as the other two. As if she had personally offended him.

"Not only a hawk shifter, he's a fucking wetback," Mason said to his friends.

Saffy's fingers shifted into claws and a hiss tore from her throat. She'd been trying to keep the cat inside her buried deep because if she let it out, even a little bit, her animal would tear shreds out of Mason for daring to call her mate that horrible name. And if she attacked her brother, her already precarious situation would get a damn sight worse—she couldn't fight the three of them together. In honesty, she didn't like her chances of taking just Mason, but if he didn't watch his mouth she'd be willing to give it a shot. Either way, at this rate it wasn't going to be her decision. There was only so much she could take before her cat tried to force its way out.

"Who the fuck is that now?" Mason asked with a frown.

Huh?

What had she missed?

Mason transferred the bottle to his other hand then reached into the back pocket of his jeans and pulled out his cellphone. He swiped his thumb over the screen to pick up a call, and put the cell to his ear.

"Lo," he answered.

Mason was only standing a few feet from her so Saffy could hear every word from the call.

"Mason, where are you? The hawk shifter is here and he's arguing with dad. I think they're gonna start fighting."

It was Charlotte. And she sounded scared. Saffy closed her eyes. She hated this. She didn't want her sister to be afraid. And she could only imagine how scared Ramon was when he found out her brother had taken her from the salon. And her father would be no help—his hatred of the Miguels would blind him to anything Ramon had to say.

Saffy prayed that Ramon could hold it together because as dominant male of their pride, her father was a very powerful man, and she couldn't stand the thought of what he might do to her mate. She knew he was the son of a dominant, like her, so he could undoubtedly take care of himself, but it didn't mean he'd be a match for a lion, and it certainly wouldn't be a fair fight: there was no way her father was there alone, and the rest of the pride wouldn't stand back and let a hawk insult them like that. They were honor-bound to protect the pride's territory. And whatever happened, if it came to a fight, someone she loved would be hurt. Her dad might be an overbearing, prejudiced jerk, but he was still her father.

"The fuck?" Mason said.

"He's looking for Saffy," Charlotte said. "Is she with you?"

"Be right there," Mason said before hanging up. He grinned at Saffy. "Looks like your spick boyfriend is causing trouble again. About to go and have me a little chat with him."

Saffy let out another hiss. She had never hated her brother as much in her life as she did in that very moment.

"I'm coming with you."

"Fuck no, you're staying here." He turned to his friends. "She doesn't leave this house until I get back."

Saffy made to follow him to the door, but Leon and Jason grabbed her and pulled her back.

"Get your hands off me!" she shouted.

Jason had a face like thunder, but Leon merely grinned at her.

"Mason!" she shouted. "*Mason!*"

He ignored her, slamming the front door closed behind him.

"You've only got yourself to blame," Leon said.

She threw up her hands in disbelief. "For what, meeting my mate?"

"You could have had any man you wanted," he carried on as if he hadn't heard her. "And you chose *him*."

"Jealous?" she taunted.

"*Jealous?*" he repeated. "Why the fuck would I be jealous of a fucking hawk shifter? Heard they got dicks the size of maggots."

He roared with laughter at his joke and Jason chuckled along with him.

"And I heard you've got a vagina," she snapped back.

"Shut the fuck up!" he roared. "Or I'll show you exactly what I got, and you'd probably beg me for it, too."

Saffy shook her head. "You're deluded. Now I *know* you're jealous because you've been trying to get in my pants for months, but you're too stupid to realize I find you repulsive!"

His face turned an angry shade of red, and before she even had time to question her sanity for insulting him when she was alone with him and his best friend, he drew his hand back and slammed it into her face. Hard. She staggered back into the wall, blood leaking from her re-opened lip.

"I wouldn't touch your slut, hawk-loving ass with a bargepole. You're damaged goods." He looked at the clock. "Anyway, Mason will be at your home any moment and he and your father are gonna kick the shit out of that fucking Miguel asshole. If we're lucky, they might even kill him."

Saffy's eyes widened and she to tried to duck around Leon to get to the door. He grabbed her upper arms, his fingers biting into the flesh as he swung her round and laughed in her face. She struggled to break free from his grip, but he only laughed harder at her futile attempts.

"Go on," he said. "I like a woman who fights."

Oh, he wanted a fight, did he? Fine. She'd give him one. Saffy spat in his face. He touched a finger to the glob of saliva and curled his lip in disgust. She knew right then she was in deep, deep trouble.

Chapter Eleven

Ramon

Was Ramon mistaken or was there a brief hint of respect on Owen's face?

"I've got to hand it to you," the dominant male said. "Not many men would be stupid enough to come to my home and threaten me. Or brave enough."

"She's my mate," Ramon said simply. "There's nothing I wouldn't do for her."

When Owen frowned, Ramon feared he was about to lose whatever ground he had just gained.

"She was afraid," he said quickly. "And I'm willing to bet your daughter doesn't scare easily. Please, if you have any idea where Mason would have taken her, tell me. I just want to make sure she's all right."

The man's expression softened ever so slightly around his eyes, and Ramon was just about to breathe a sigh of relief when he heard someone behind him, walking up the pathway towards the house. He turned and found himself face to face with Mason who, judging by the dopey, self-satisfied grin on his face, was inebriated. He grabbed the collar of Mason's shirt and shook him.

"Where is she?" he demanded.

"None of your goddamn business," Mason spat.

"If you want to live to see tomorrow, you'd better tell me where she is."

Anger flashed in Mason's eyes and he gripped Ramon's wrists and tried to pry them loose from his shirt, but Ramon brought all his strength to bear. He wasn't about to let Mason get away until he'd answered him.

"Where is she?" Ramon shouted again, louder this time and with real menace in his voice.

"Mason," Owen bit out. "Where's your sister?"

Mason looked up at his father and frowned, as if surprised that he seemed to be taking Ramon's side, but he recovered quickly, his gaze returning to Ramon.

"If you come with me, I'll take you to her."

"Why, so you and your friends can kick the shit out of me?" Ramon said. "You don't think you could take me on your own?" He shrugged and released him. "Bring it on, I'm not afraid of any of you."

Mason grinned and was just about to turn to head back down the pathway when his father caught his attention.

"Just how much have you had to drink today?" he asked.

"Hardly anything," Mason said.

Ramon knew it was a lie, not only because of what his mate had told him on the phone earlier but because Mason smelled like a brewery. Alcohol was seeping out of his every pore, and that was without the glazed expression and the red, rheumy eyes. Ramon started to follow Mason down the pathway when Owen said, "Wait up, I'm coming too."

Mason spun around. "What the hell?"

Owen's face turned a surprising shade of red. "Don't you *dare* speak to me like that," he snapped. "I am your father and your dominant. I want to know why Saffy was upset earlier, and I want to hear what she's got to say about you scaring her customers at the salon today."

Mason's face blanched, but he was smart enough to keep his mouth shut. He did, however, glare at Ramon for ratting him out before he headed on his way. Ramon started to breathe a sigh of relief. Saffy had to be okay if

Mason was prepared to take his father to where he was keeping her, but if she was okay, why hadn't she called him back? He'd left her several messages and a dozen missed calls.

Of course, it could all have been a ruse so that Mason, his friends, plus Owen could attack him when they got to wherever they were going, but Ramon didn't think it likely. Owen Brown had risen to the rank of dominant and held it for a lot of years. He didn't strike Ramon as the type of man who needed anyone else to do his dirty work for him. If he had wanted to attack him, he would have done it on his doorstep earlier when Ramon had been shouting at him. Ramon could only assume he hadn't because he was Saffy's mate. Perhaps it meant there was some hope that Owen might be able to accept their relationship, one day in the not-too-distant future. But first, Ramon had to get his mate back.

They headed along the sidewalk, far too slowly for Ramon's liking. It was all he could do to keep from tracking Mason's scent back to the house at a sprint, and kicking down the door to wherever he'd taken her.

If Mason kept dragging his feet, Ramon was going to throttle him, and he didn't imagine his father would have much to say about it either, based on the glares Owen kept throwing his son. It seemed to take hours to reach a house about half a block away from the Brown household.

"You brought her to Leon's house?" Owen said, narrowing his eyes. Mason grunted a reply. "Where's the rest of the family—I assume they didn't go along with this?"

"Fort Lauderdale."

Ramon bit down hard on his tongue as fury boiled in his stomach. Mason had left her alone with his loser friends. Saffy hadn't had to spell it out, he'd seen her around them at the party and it was obvious they made her uncomfortable. If she didn't trust them, he didn't, either, and it took all his self-control to keep himself from shouting at Mason to hurry the hell up and get in the house so that he could see his mate. Perhaps Mason wouldn't have hurt his sister, but could the same be said about his friends?

The front door to the house was unlocked. Mason opened it then led the way inside. Ramon followed him in with Owen bringing up the rear. Mason stopped dead just inside the living room, blocking the doorway so Ramon couldn't get inside.

"What the hell?" Mason asked.

"Mason," one of his friends said. Ramon thought it was Leon. "I…I can explain. She wouldn't fucking sh—"

Ramon gave Mason a shove that sent him flying into the room and burst in after him. Then it was his turn to come to a standstill as he tried to process what he was seeing. Saffy was lying prone on the floor, her lip split open. A bruise was forming on her cheek. But the worst thing was how still she was lying. Completely unmoving. She didn't even appear to be breathing. Was she d—? He couldn't even think the word.

Ramon let out an unearthly roar then charged into the room, flying at Mason's friends. He punched Jason with an uppercut that sent him flying back into a cabinet, the glass in the front of it exploding as he crashed into it, and then crumpled to the floor in a heap.

Without even pausing to draw breath, Ramon rounded on Leon, who was still standing over Saffy's body. The lion shifter paled and started to raise his hands, either to defend himself or fight back but Ramon didn't give him the chance. He slammed his fist into Leon's face then did it again. Leon fell back against the wall and Ramon rounded on him. He hit him again. After he heard the man's nose breaking, he drew his fist back and punched him again.

"Ramon!" someone called.

Ramon didn't listen. There was no room in his mind for anything else other than the knowledge that this man had hurt his mate. For that he would suffer, as she had.

Oh God, was she—? He swallowed, and then bared his teeth, his hawk urging him on.

"Ramon!" someone called again. "Jesus, Mason, help me grab him."

It was only when Ramon was dragged back that he realized it was only his repeated punches that had been keeping Leon upright. As soon as he was pulled away, the lion shifter who'd dared touch his mate hit the floor like a ton of bricks. Ramon was turned around by the hands hold him to stare into the face of Owen Brown.

"See to your mate," Owen ordered.

The words brought some sort of semblance of sanity back to Ramon's mind and he looked down to where Saffy was lying, looking so fragile and still. He choked out a sob then fell to his knees beside her. Then, some of his

FBI training kicked in and he checked her vitals. It was the longest second of his life before he felt her lifeforce pressing back against his fingers. She was alive and her pulse was strong.

She was alive.

Ramon lifted Saffy's body and cradled her against his chest, rocking slightly.

"Baby, wake up," he said gently, stroking the side of her face and the top of her head. "I've got you. Wake up."

When she failed to open her eyes, Ramon kept murmuring to her softly, running his hands down her cheek and neck. A tear slid down his cheek as he pleaded with her and urged her to wake, to look at him, to come back to him. It was several long moments of pure agony and terror before her eyelashes flickered and she slowly opened her eyes, blinking and trying to focus on Ramon's face. She was evidently disoriented, but his heart swelled with pride to see her doing her best to shake it off.

"Ramon? What happened?" she asked at last.

Ramon frowned. "You don't remember?"

She tried to get up into a sitting position and look around to get her bearings. Her eyes widened when she caught sight of Jason and Leon lying on the living room floor just a few feet away from her. She lifted her gaze to Ramon's.

"Did you do all that?" she asked.

Ramon nodded.

"My hero," she said, making him smile. "You came for me."

Ramon stroked her hair away from the side of her face, near to where a large purple bruise was forming. "Of course I came for you. You're my mate—I'll always come for you. I only wish I could have got to you sooner. Can you ever forgive me?"

She shook her head then winced. "There's nothing to forgive. This wasn't your fault."

Ramon glared at Mason who was standing quietly nearby with his father, all the fight seeming to have left him. "No," he said. "We know whose fault it was."

It in no way made up for what he'd done, but Mason looked contrite, his gaze shifting between Ramon and Saffy.

"I'm sorry," he breathed. "I never wanted you to get hurt."

Ramon simply stared at him, unwilling at that moment in time to accept the apology. His actions had caused all of this, caused his mate to be terrified and hurt, and there were no mere words that could make up for it.

Saffy followed Ramon's gaze and her eyes widened again. "Dad?"

Owen opened his mouth to say something when movement from the floor near them caught their attention. Leon groaned and Jason pushed himself up into a sitting position. Owen walked over to them, looming above them menacingly.

"You're out of the pride," he said, his voice as cold and detached as Ramon had ever heard it. "Banished. After today, I never want to see either of your faces again."

Jason let out a surprised gasp, but Leon didn't utter a single word, not that there was anything he could have said after everything he had done. Owen rounded on his son.

"I should banish you too, after pulling a stunt like this, but you can count this as your final warning. You're on probation. If you don't stop drinking, clean up your act, and find a job in the next three months, you're gone, too."

The fear that bled into Mason's expression seemed genuine enough, but Ramon couldn't help but wonder if the dominant would make good on his threat if Mason didn't do what was required of him.

Owen looked down at Saffy and Ramon and a tiny little bit of compassion stole over his face.

"My deepest apologies," he said to Saffy. "To you and your mate. This is my fault and I take full responsibility. If I hadn't reacted to your mating the way I had and thrown you out of the house, none of this would have happened. I'm very sorry. I hope one day you can find it in your heart to forgive me."

Ramon nearly choked on his surprise, but he hid it from Owen and from his mate.

Saffy looked as if she was trying to hold back her tears. "I forgive you, Daddy."

She didn't say a word to her brother which made Ramon wonder what had gone on between them before he got there. He looked down at her.

"Do you think you can stand?"

When she nodded, he helped her get to her feet and as he led her from the house, he didn't spare a backwards glance at any of them. Saffy might have forgiven her father, but Ramon couldn't find it in his heart to do the same. Not yet, anyway, but perhaps he would be able to forgive him in the future.

He put his arms around Saffy's shoulder.

"Let's get you home," he said to her.

"Thank you," she replied, leaning into his side. "Home sounds great right about now."

Chapter Twelve

Saffy

When Saffy opened her eyes, she was lying in bed, a warm solid presence at her back and it only took her a moment to realize what it was. Ramon was pressed up against her, his arm wrapped around her waist and one of his legs thrown over both of hers. He had essentially trapped her in the bed, but she'd never felt safer or more comfortable and a small smile slid over her lips. If this was being trapped, she never wanted to be free.

"Good morning beautiful," he said, pulling her even tighter against his chest.

"You're awake."

"Yeah, for about thirty minutes now."

She frowned. "Why didn't you get up?"

"I did," he said. "I went to call your boss to tell her you wouldn't be in today then I called mine and gave him the same news."

"Thank you," she murmured into his muscular chest. "I don't feel up to working today and I probably would have scared the customers away with my black eye."

"It's healing well," Ramon said.

"Thank God."

She'd shifted when they got home the night before to help her body heal from her injuries, but it would take another day at least for her bruises to disappear.

"You didn't need to take the day off yourself," she said. "I'd have been fine here on my own."

"I did," he said.

"Why?"

"Gonna spend it spoiling you."

Saffy smiled. She liked the sound of that. Very much.

"Why didn't you wake me?"

"After what you went through yesterday, I figured you deserved a lie in."

She heaved a sigh. "I'm fine, honestly. You don't need to worry."

"I might not need to, but I'm going to. It's my job to worry about you, mi cielo."

She sighed again and snuggled closer to Ramon's front. "Did I tell you I like it when you speak Spanish to me?"

At that, Ramon leaned in close to her ear and started murmuring to her softly in Spanish. She recognized a couple of the words, so was able to get the gist of what he said, but she wished she could understand all of it.

"Hmm," she said, after he'd finished talking. "You're going to have to teach me."

"Yeah, you want to learn?"

"Definitely."

She turned in his arms then placed a long, lingering kiss on his lips. When the kiss began to get heated, Ramon started to pull away.

"I think we should wait until you're fully healed."

"I took a couple of punches, I didn't break any bones." She rolled her eyes. "I'm not sure if you noticed, but I *am* a lion shifter. I'm not fragile—I won't shatter if you touch me."

"You were knocked unconscious," he said, a dark shadow bleeding into his expression. "You might have had a concussion. I just think we should wait until…"

"You can do all the work," she said, waggling her eyebrows at him. "I'll just lie here perfectly still. Won't move a muscle."

Ramon's shoulders started shaking with his laughter. "Mamita," he said after his hilarity had subsided. "If that's your best effort at seducing me…"

"I didn't realize I *needed* to seduce you," she said. "But if that's what it takes."

She leaned forward and kissed him again, and at the same time, reached between them and pressed the palm of her hand against the front of Ramon's boxers. He groaned against her mouth and as the kiss wore on, it got more and more heated, and Ramon hardened to her touch. He groaned again then rolled them so that she was flat on her back and he was lying over her, weight braced on his arms so that there was just the barest whisper of air between them.

"Okay, okay, you win," he said against her lips, much to her amusement and delight.

She slid her hands down his back and into the waistband of his boxers before sliding them over the cheeks of his ass. He helped her remove them before pulling down her panties and tossing them over his shoulder. When he came back, his head went to her sex and he closed his mouth over her clit and sucked then flicked it with his tongue.

"Oh!" she groaned, her back arching off the bed.

Ramon stopped what he was doing then lifted his head to meet her gaze. "I thought you said you weren't going to move."

She grinned down at him. "Umm, sorry?"

He shook his head, smiling wryly before getting back to work with his mouth. Then he brought his fingers into the mix, torturing her by bringing her almost to the brink then backing off before she came.

"What are you doing?" she asked when he stopped his ministrations completely to move up and over her body.

He grinned down at her wickedly. "Callate, mi amor. Just feel."

He kissed her again, his mouth surprisingly gentle and his hardness settled between her legs. Saffy groaned and opened her thighs wider to better accommodate him. The kiss was as tender and light as any they had ever shared. Until then, their lovemaking had been fast and frantic, but this was anything but. It seemed as if Ramon *was* treating her as if she was fragile, but she was enjoying this new side of him so much, she couldn't bring herself to call him on it.

They were sharing a new intimacy that she was only too happy to explore, and his kisses were producing an unexpected, but eager response from her body. She grew impossibly wet and when he finally slid into her, it was with the same beautiful but aching slowness as his intoxicating kisses. He started moving in her with a slow, gentle rhythm. She lifted her legs and wrapped them around his hips, and he rocked into her with a tenderness that electrified her. There was no urgency to their movements, and yet it was as erotic and as passionate as any of the times they had come together previously. More so, even, if that was possible.

Ramon leaned up on his elbows above her and stared down into her eyes and as they continued to move their hips in a slow, erotic dance, they didn't break eye contact for a single second. She moaned aloud as her entire body flooded with desire, her breathing sped and her heart raced, and when her orgasm finally hit, it lingered on and on, intensifying when Ramon found his own release, and stilled deep inside her, her name sounding like a benediction as it fell from his lips.

Afterward as they lay together in the cradle of each other's arms, Saffy's mouth stretched into a grin.

"It seems I need to offer to lay still and not do any work every time we—"

"Don't even think about it," Ramon said sternly, making a light, carefree laugh spill from her lips.

Chapter Thirteen

Ramon

Ramon scrubbed his sweaty palms down the thighs of his jeans as he led Saffy up the steps to the porch of his parents' house. He had called his mom earlier that morning to say he was coming over to dinner that night and would be bringing a guest with him, but he hadn't told her who he was bringing. He figured that was something that would be better done face to face. Saffy watched him wipe his hands and frowned.

"You're making me nervous," she said, under her breath. "Relax. What's the worst that can happen?"

He didn't want to think about the worst thing that could happen, but images of his father telling him to get out and to never set foot inside the house again ran through his mind regardless. And after everything Saffy had just been through with her own family, he hated the thought she might face any sort of rejection from his. Maybe this had been a mistake. Maybe he should have told his family on his own, and spared her from facing whatever their reaction would be. But it was too late now. He stopped outside the door and sucked in a deep breath.

Saffy pulled him to a stop just as his hand was raised to open the front door.

"Whatever happens in there, we'll get through it together, okay?"

Feeling suddenly choked with emotion, Ramon pulled his mate into his arms and kissed her long and hard.

"I don't deserve you," he said when they pulled apart.

"It's funny," she said, "But I feel exactly the same way about you."

He offered her a reassuring smile. "Okay. Let's do this."

His mom and dad always left the front door unlocked so Ramon pressed on the handle and the door opened. As soon as he stepped foot into the hallway, his mother was there, pulling him down for a kiss on the cheek.

"Mi hijo," she said warmly. "I missed you."

Ramon chuckled. "You just saw me the other day, Mama."

"Is too long," she said.

Then her eyes drifted to over Ramon's shoulder and they widened. "Who is your friend?"

Ramon opened his mouth to reply, and it was at that moment that his father chose to come out into the hallway. "What's going on out here? The tamales are getting cold."

His father surveyed the scene then his eyes landed on Saffy. His nose twitched as he scented the air and Ramon saw that his mother was doing the same thing.

Ramon's father turned to him with a frown. "A lion shifter? Ramon, what's going on here?"

Ramon pulled in a deep, calming breath then reached out to put his hand around Saffy's shoulder. "Mom, dad, this is Saffy, my mate."

His father looked on with genuine confusion, but his mother's face lit up with what could only be described as glee.

"Ramon?" she questioned. "You met your mate?"

He nodded. "Yes, Mama."

His mother stumbled forward, and Ramon waited with bated breath for what she would say—he was too afraid to look at his father's reaction.

His mother came to a stop in front of Saffy then reached up, grabbed hold of her face and dragged her down for a big old kiss right on the lips. When she let her go, she was still smiling brightly and Saffy looked a little shell shocked by the open display of affection.

"Mi hija," his mother said. *My daughter.* "It's so good to meet you."

"Pleased to meet you, too," Saffy returned after a stunned moment.

It was then that Ramon glanced at his father. The confusion he'd seen earlier had disappeared from his face to be replaced with surprise and curiosity. He'd take it—it was better than open hostility. Better than he'd dared to hope for.

"How is this possible?" his father asked. "It's like history repeating itself."

His mother looked over her shoulder and glared at her husband.

"Carlos," she said sternly. "Greet your new daughter properly."

Ramon's dad threw his mother a look of long-suffering exasperation, that somehow managed to be full of affection. It was a look that he had seen on his father's face hundreds of times in the past. Then his father stepped forward and took hold of Saffy's hand.

"This has come as quite the surprise," he said. "As I'm sure it did for you, too. Nonetheless, welcome to my home, and welcome to my family, my daughter."

"Thank you, sir," she whispered. "That means a lot to me."

When tears filled his mate's eyes, a lump rose in Ramon's throat. He'd never been prouder to be called a Miguel and he'd never been prouder of his parents.

"Thank you," he said, struggling to speak around the lump in his throat. "Your acceptance means the world to me."

His mom looked at him as if he'd lost his mind.

"Why wouldn't we accept it? Saffy is your soul mate. It's fate. That means she's part of our family now, too."

As his mother led the way into the dining room, Ramon slid his hand into Saffy's and squeezed it gently, but he wasn't sure if he did it to offer her comfort or because he needed it himself—probably a little bit of both. He only wished he had told his parents as soon as he and Saffy had met, then he could have called on his father to go to the salon when Mason and his friends had showed up. Perhaps then, she wouldn't have got hurt. He should have trusted his parents to be as accepting and welcoming as he'd always known them to be. He hated that the reaction from Saffy's parents had got him running scared and made him question how his own parents would react.

When he walked into the dining room, Ramon stopped short just inside the door.

"Where is everyone?" he asked.

His mother's table was always full and as she knew Ramon was coming over, he had expected her to invite his brother and sister, their children, plus a handful of cousins. He'd never known their dining room to be so devoid of people.

"You told us you were bringing someone to dinner," his mother said.

Ramon blinked. "Right. I would have thought you'd use that as an excuse to throw a party."

She shared a glance with her husband then met Ramon's gaze again. "You were secretive, so we think you were bringing a man to dinner and going to tell us you're gay. I welcome my new son, of course, but we didn't think you want an audience for that if you so secretive about it."

"*Gay?*" Ramon spluttered. "Whatever made you think that?"

His mother shrugged. "You never bring a woman home to meet your mama." Her smile got impossibly huge. "Now you can give me lots of grandbabies."

His mother.

Ramon shook his head, exasperated, but when he turned to look at his mate, her shoulders were shaking with silent laughter, and her hand was covering what he was certain was a broad grin. He was pleased she saw the humor in the situation. He couldn't help it, he threw his head back and joined her, laughing long and hard.

Then they sat down and ate dinner. It was divine.

Tamales really were his favorite meal.

Epilogue

Saffy

It had been nearly two weeks since her brother and his friends had kidnapped her and during that time, Saffy hadn't seen hide nor hair of him or her father. Her mom had called her a couple of times, and she had spoken to her sister often. She knew things couldn't go back to the way they were, not after everything that had happened between them, but she was grateful that at least her mother wasn't hanging up on her now and she was finally allowed to speak to her sister.

Her mom had said she was welcome in their home again, and said that her father missed her, but he had yet to talk to her on the phone himself. So, it had come as a huge shock when her mom called to say her father wanted her to come to dinner. Not only that, he wanted her to invite Ramon, and Ramon's parents too. Saffy had thought hell would freeze over before her father ever sat down to eat with Miguels.

Ramon ducked his head into the bathroom. "You ready?" he asked. "My parents will be here any minute."

Her eyes widened.

"Oh my God, really? I haven't done my make up."

Ramon grinned. "Would it help if I said you're beautiful as you are?"

She shook her head. "Not really, no."

He let out a throaty chuckle. "Then you have…" He checked his watch. "Four minutes and counting to put it on. Mama insists on being punctual."

Saffy let out a little scream then all but pushed Ramon out of the door so that she could put the four minutes to good use. She touched her face where the bruises had been. They had long since healed, but the memory of them and of that day lingered and she wasn't looking forward to seeing her brother again at dinner. If she was being honest with herself, she probably wouldn't have cared if she never saw him again. Mason had scared her, probably even more than his friends had for the very reason that he was her brother, and family were supposed to protect one another.

She looked down at her make up bag and sighed. There wasn't a lot she could do in under four minutes, so she just pulled out her mascara, brushed a little through her lashes then added some clear lip gloss. That would have to do. A horn honked outside just as she was walking into the living room.

Ramon leaned in and gave her a peck on the lips. "You ready to do this?"

She shrugged. "As I'll ever be."

"Whatever happens, we'll get through it together, okay?" Ramon said, repeating the words she'd said to him at his parents' house back to her.

She smiled at him. "I don't doubt it for a second."

His eyes got soft then and he leaned in and gave her another kiss.

She grabbed her purse then they headed out to the car. Ramon's mother got out and greeted her by giving her a big kiss on the lips again then pulled Ramon down for more of the same treatment. At first, Saffy had been startled by how affectionate Ramon's mom was to someone she didn't know, but she had quickly got used to it and now, it didn't bother her in the least. His family really had accepted her into their heart, as if she'd been a part of it her whole life. They pulled away from the curb and though Ramon's mother kept up a constant stream of conversation, Saffy got more and more nervous the nearer they got to her house.

As if he could sense the change in her, Ramon reached across the seat and took hold of her hand. It calmed her instantly, and she offered him a grateful smile that fluttered over her lips like an anxious sparrow. He squeezed her hand and her breath caught. She couldn't believe how much this man had come to mean to her in such a short space of time. It was as if her entire world centered around him now. That should have terrified her, but it didn't. Being with Ramon made her feel safe and protected and cherished—exactly how a mate was supposed to make their other half feel. Hearts and flowers. Romance. It was what she'd always dreamed, and so, so much more.

Saffy had watched mated couples interact so many times in the past and had longed to have that same connection with someone. Now she had it, and she couldn't have been happier. Whatever happened, they really would get through it. Together.

When Ramon's father pulled into her street, she directed him to her house. "You can pull up into the driveway," she told him.

As soon as they had parked, the front door opened, and her mom and dad came outside to greet them.

"My baby," her mom said, pulling Saffy into a hug. "It's so good to see you."

"Hey, Mom," Saffy said, and heat prickled at her eyes.

She hadn't realized until that very moment just how much she'd missed her.

Then her mom turned to Ramon and his parents. "It's very nice to meet you," she said with surprising warmth. "Welcome to my home."

She shook hands with them both before standing aside so that her husband could greet them.

"Saffy," her dad said with a nod.

She supposed it was better than nothing.

Her father's face didn't have her mother's warmth in it, but he reached out and shook Ramon's parents' hands before shaking Ramon's.

"Please, come inside," he said and led them into the house.

After they'd taken their seats, Saffy noted that the table had been set for six. She glanced at the empty seats with a frown. "Aren't Charlotte and Mason joining us?"

Her mother shook her head. "Mason is working, and Charlotte is at her friend's birthday party."

Huh, her sister hadn't told her about the party. Then the rest of what her mother had said sunk in and her eyes widened.

"Mason has a *job*?" she spluttered.

She glanced at her mate and noted the surprise on his face, too.

Her mom nodded. "Security, though why he couldn't put that expensive college degree to good use is beyond me."

"Mason has actually started to make some changes for the better," her father said. "With those horrible boys he used to hang around with gone, I think he might just be able to turn his life around. He has stop drinking and is far more agreeable company now."

Saffy would believe it when she saw it. It was true, his friends hadn't been very nice, in fact they *had* been horrible, but Mason had been the ringleader of their little group, there was no doubt about it. She wasn't sure she liked the way her father made them out to be the bad guys and she hoped it didn't mean he go easy on Mason and allow him to slip back into his old ways.

"Do you have more children?" her mom asked Ramon's mother, moving onto a safe topic for them both

Ramon's mom smiled and nodded, moving her hands animatedly as she spoke. "Si, three in total, two boys and a girl."

Her parents made a little small talk until the server that her mom had hired for the night brought out the first course. Dinner was a stuffy affair, nothing like the relaxed, comfortable atmosphere at Ramon's parents' house, but at least her parents were civil. More actually, they could even have been described as friendly.

After the meal was finished, her father opened a bottle of champagne and shared it out between six flutes before handing a glass to each of them and taking one for himself.

"I do hope you'll join me in congratulating Saffy and Ramon on their mating," he said, to her surprise. "I'm sure you'll agree that our families have been at war for too long and I hope that our children's mating can bring an end to the feud, once and for all."

He raised his glass in a toast. "To Saffy and Ramon!"

"To Saffy and Ramon," their parents said in unison before they all drank to the toast.

A glance at Ramon told her that he was just as surprised by her father's toast and request for an end to the feud as she was.

"I will happily agree to a truce," Ramon's dad said. "If we both agree to enforce it by threat of banishment. Many of the younger generation don't know what started it in the first place and I think they would be more than happy to see it come to an end."

"I can agree to that," her father said.

She doubted her brother would be happy about it, but Saffy kept quiet about that. Perhaps she was being too hard on Mason. There was a chance that he did want to turn his life around for the better. She supposed only time would tell.

"To Ramon and Saffy," Ramon's father said. "Thank you for finding each other and for bringing our two families together so that we can put aside our differences and live in peace once again."

As Saffy raised her glass, she caught the happiness in Ramon's expression and knew it mirrored the look she wore on her own face.

"To Ramon and Saffy," her mom said. "May your future be bright."

"And may you give us lots of grandbabies as soon as possible," Ramon's mom added.

They all laughed then drank their toast to the couple who Saffy would have been only too quick to describe as deliriously happy. Their mating may not have gotten off to the start many shifters dreamed of, but she couldn't imagine that any other couple could be happier than they were in that moment—and would be, for every moment, for the rest of their lives together. She had everything she'd ever dreamed of. Hearts, flowers, romance—all of that. But most importantly, she had Ramon. Her mate.

A note from the author

Thanks so much for taking the time to read HELD BY THE HAWK. I hope you enjoyed falling in love with Ramon and Saffy as much as I did. Be sure to check out Sloane's story in PRIZED BY THE POLAR BEAR, available from your favorite book seller now, or by scanning the QR code below.

For latest updates and releases, check out my Facebook page
www.facebook.com/AuthorBellaDrake

Printed in Great Britain
by Amazon